My Home, Sweet Home

Giovanni Guareschi is the author of

THE LITTLE WORLD OF DON CAMILLO

COMRADE DON CAMILLO

MY HOME, SWEET HOME

MY HOME, SWEET HOME

Giovanni Guareschi

FARRAR, STRAUS AND GIROUX

NEW YORK

Contents

PREAMBLE

Why do I go on talking about myself?

Who am I?

Am I so important a man as to excite people's interest and make them eager to hear even the minutest details of my family life?

Certainly not. I'm an ordinary man. And that's why it seems to me, as I speak of me and mine, that I am telling a bit of the story of millions and millions of ordinary men— who in their wise ordinariness keep our poor old shanty of a world standing where "exceptional" men, men who are "out of the ordinary," men of genius, would be more likely to tear it down.

Why do I keep talking about myself, about Margherita, and Albertino, and the Pasionaria?

It's only fair, that's why. History and chronicle are preoccupied with communicating to contemporaries and handing down to posterity the doings of "exceptional" men—but no one pays the slightest attention to ordinary men.

And who are Giovannino, Margherita, Albertino, and the Pasionaria if not representatives of the "ordinary" family?

What difference does it make if Margherita has a tomato complex? If Albertino is obsessed with the sex of bicycles? If the Pasionaria would rather have a bottle-capping machine than the most beautiful doll in the world? If I, Giovannino, have the job I have and wear the mustache I wear?

There is, truly, nothing "exceptional" in all this, and my family is not an "original" family, and Margherita is not an "unusual" woman. Neither are Albertino and the Pasionaria "extraordinary" children. . . .

There are a hundred different varieties of grape—from white to black, from sweet to sour, from small to large. But if you press a hundred bunches of grapes of different varieties, the juice is always wine. If you squeeze grapes, you never get gasoline, milk, or lemonade.

And it's the juice that counts—in everything.

And the juice of my family is the same as the juice of millions of "ordinary" families, because the basic problems of my family are the same as those of millions of families: they spring from a family situation based on the necessity of adhering to the principles that are the foundation of all "ordinary" homes.

Of all honest homes, in short.

Why am I always talking about me and the people in my house? In order to talk about you and the people in your house. To console both you and me for the boring lives we lead, the lives of honest, ordinary people. To smile with you at our little daily troubles. To take from those little troubles (little even when they're big) the dark hue of tragedy they so often assume if kept bottled up within ourselves.

So there it is. If I have a problem, I rid myself of it by confiding it to the *Corrierino*. And those among the readers of the *Corrierino* who have a problem deep in their hearts may also, when they read about it in detail in the columns of the *Corrierino*, feel freed of it.

From a strictly personal problem it thus becomes universal.

And quite a different thing.

The Author

HEIRS

There's a little game that mamas dearly love and that often enlivens family evenings.

The father sits reading his newspaper, the children are playing quietly on the floor. The lady of the house looks far into the distance, beyond the walls, beyond life itself. Time passes; she sighs.

"One of these days," she murmurs in a low voice, "I won't be with you any more . . ."

The children, alarmed, raise their heads.

"One of these days," the lady of the house goes on, her voice pained, ever so subtly, ever so bitterly pained, "one of these days I won't be with you any more, I'll be buried in the cold earth."

The children begin to worry.

"Your poor mama," moans the lady of the house, "your poor old mama, alone in the cemetery, the sad, silent cemetery . . ."

The children hold their breath, their eyes filled with tears.

"And in winter"—she sighs again—"it will snow, and the cold snow will cover your poor mama's grave."

The cold snow, that detail of the cold snow, plunges the unhappy children into deepest depression, and they burst into loud sobs, and they run wailing to kiss their poor mama, who by this time is so immersed in the game she feels herself to be quite thoroughly dead.

"My poor little orphans!" she cries. "Who'll tuck you in at night? Ah, will you remember your poor mama once in a while?"

The children's sobs grow louder.

"And will you come sometimes and bring flowers to my grave?"

The little orphans are howling now but their mama has no pity for them.

"When I die, I'll leave this watch to *you,* and to *you* I'll leave my gold chain . . ."

Yes, this is a game women like to play. And among Margherita's other serious defects is that of being a woman.

I remember an evening in April. It was raining, and Margherita had been playing the game. The Pasionaria, sitting with her legs tucked under her, was sobbing. Albertino was sobbing too, as he read the latest Donald Duck episode.

"I'll leave my bicycle to you," Margherita said to the Pasionaria.

"What about me?" sobbed Albertino. "Don't I get a bicycle too?"

"Mama's is a woman's bicycle," sobbed the Pasionaria. "And two can't go on it because it hasn't got a bar in the middle. Anyway, you'll have Papa's bicycle when Papa dies."

"But what if Papa doesn't die?" sobbed Albertino, reading his comic book in deep despair.

I had now been brought into it, but I paid no attention,

and there followed some moments of anxious waiting, broken only by the sobs of the two orphans.

"Giovannino," said Margherita in a tone of tender reproach, "for once in your life be nice, will you? Have you no consideration for a poor dead woman? Are you going to go on making me worry even as I lie in my grave? Making me wonder whether my two precious orphans are quarreling over a miserable bicycle!"

I have always had the greatest respect for corpses.

"Okay," I said to Albertino, "when I die, I'll leave you my bicycle."

"Thanks," sobbed Albertino, not raising his head from his comic book. "And the Guzzi 65 motorcycle too?"

"Certainly," I replied. "The Guzzi 65 too."

Then the Pasionaria raised her plaintive voice.

"He gets the motorcycle," she wailed, "and I don't get anything. I'm the youngest and I have to walk while he rides."

Margherita broke in. "How can you be such a little liar? Haven't you got my bicycle already?"

"Yes, but even on a bike you have to use your feet," the Pasionaria sobbed. "I want the motorcycle."

A somewhat acrimonious discussion followed between Margherita and the Pasionaria as to whether it was or was not suitable for a girl to ride a motorcycle. The conclusion was that, according to the Pasionaria, if a woman can drive a car with four wheels she can just as well drive a motorcycle with two.

I sought to find a compromise. "I'll leave the motorcycle to the two of you. Albertino can drive and you can ride in the back."

The Pasionaria accepted.

"But the goggles," she whimpered, "go to me."

Here Albertino intervened. As the driver of the motor-cycle, he felt, he had the right to the goggles. It was a sound argument, but the Pasionaria was determined to hold on to her victory.

"All right, all right," I said. "I'll buy another pair."

Albertino then politely turned to the disposition of my camera. But Margherita rebelled.

"That's enough!" she cried. "Have a little respect for your poor father's dead body! There's nothing worse than haggling over a dead man while he's still alive!"

Albertino and the Pasionaria went reluctantly to bed. When we were alone, Margherita lit a cigarette and sighed: "A funny business, this. A person doesn't have a chance to get used to living before he has to start getting used to dying. We're on a little path cut into the over-hanging rock and we're trying desperately to hold on to earth, but we're fascinated by the abyss—by eternity. And every so often we feel we have to look down into that abyss."

"Yes," I said, "and we pay no attention to the sign on the edge of the precipice saying it's dangerous to lean out over the side."

One day my favorite jacket showed me that even the best of jackets have their Achilles' heel in the elbow. So I took my brown corduroy jacket out of the wardrobe, and discovered that a little green disk had been attached to it just below the collar.

It didn't bother me too much, and I wasn't alarmed

even after I found another green paper circle glued inside a shoe. Later, when I found still another green disk stuck on the side of my typewriter, I began to wonder.

I found a green disk fastened to the underside of one of the chairs in my workroom. I examined another chair and found a red circle fastened to that one.

Thumbing through a new reference work, I found a green disk in the first volume (language section) and a red disk on the cover of the second volume (science section). At about this time, Margherita found, under the folding top of the kitchen stove, two disks side by side: a red one and a green one.

Then Margherita found red circles on her dresses, and I found green circles almost everywhere. Very soon there wasn't a single object in our house that wasn't marked in either red or green or both.

Finally, going through my wallet, I came across a red disk on my identity card and a green disk on my driver's license and my gun permit. A red disk and a green disk were stuck on the 10,000 lire note that happened at that time to be in my wallet.

Even the handkerchief I pulled out of my pocket to wipe my sweating brow had a little green circle glued on a corner.

Something was going on.

"It's like living in a detective story," said Margherita one day. And her eyes opened wide as she discovered a red disk on the bottom of the coffee grinder she was holding in her hand.

Margherita said we were being persecuted by some secret crime society with political overtones. One day we would learn the meaning of those fearful red and green warnings: and maybe it would be too late.

But I had my own ideas on the subject and remained calm. I've had considerable experience with affairs of a mysterious nature, having written some thirty radio dramas, all quite complicated, with trials by jury and psychological problems and such. So I decided to follow the trail and one night got quietly out of bed and made my way on silent feet like a ghost to my workroom. The lights were on, and I was able to observe the secret society at work. They weren't all there—only half the forces were present, and this half was sticking a red disk on a corner of my compass case.

The Pasionaria was not intimidated: she motioned to me not to make any noise.

"There was a green sticker there already," she explained. "I pulled it off and put a red one on. Now this goes to me."

For the author of thirty radio dramas with a jury of the people, solving this crime was not very difficult: they had agreed to split their inheritance. Albertino affixed green disks on what had been left to him; the Pasionaria put red disks on what had been left to her. The Pasionaria, working on her own, was now fraudulently taking possession of the compass that had by common consent been left to Albertino.

I gave the Pasionaria a stern look and delivered a long, impassioned discourse. The Pasionaria at last lowered her head in shame. Then after a moment she went to the desk, fumbled around it, and jumped on a chair and stuck a little red disk right in the middle of my forehead.

Her property.

I had no idea what to say, so I went back to bed with the red stamp proudly affixed to my forehead.

Margherita was asleep, dreaming dreams invented by Edgar Allan Poe. On a corner of her pillow was a green sticker.

It's dangerous to lean out over the side, Margherita.

A BRAND-NAME LADDER

I was born before the First World War, around the time of the Messina earthquake. Yet I didn't know until a few days ago that a brand-name ladder can cost 24,730 lire. I only knew that when I wanted to drive a nail high in the wall or get the *Domenica del Corriere* for 1899 down from the bookshelves, I had to construct an outlandish battlement of chairs and tables.

Then a few days ago I saw a handsome six-rung wooden ladder—the folding kind that opens to stand by itself—and I thought in my innocence that it would be a good thing to buy. I was encouraged by having the Pasionaria with me. She had examined the ladder exhaustively and was quite satisfied with it.

"It's okay," she said. "It'll be fine for playing 'good

morning, signora, now I have to go upstairs and cook lunch.'"

Confronted by so cogent an argument, I asked the owner of the shop to send me the ladder, and when it arrived, I paid 24,730 lire for it. That includes 720 lire for national sales tax and 10 lire for local sales tax, for even ladders have to help balance the budget.

Margherita was there when I paid the bill and she was quite calm. She just wanted to know if the ladder worked on electricity or on gas. I explained that it worked like all ladders, even non-brand-name ones. It had no mechanism so you could go up and down automatically merely by pressing a button, I said. And at this a look of great sadness came over her face.

"Wars have to be paid for even when lost," I told Margherita. And Margherita shook her head mournfully, brightening only when I informed her the ladder was made of *steamed* beech.

"A steam ladder!" Margherita cried. "Then it *is* mechanical!"

We put the ladder in the middle of our largest room and I mounted—at 4121.66 lire each—the six rungs.

Margherita, the Pasionaria, and Albertino watched respectfully.

"Giovannino," gasped Margherita, "seen this way from below, you seem to be looking off into the future. And how small and fragile I must look to you, from up above!"

Raising my arm, I touched the ceiling. I shifted my weight, I stood on one foot, I jiggled the brand-name ladder, but there wasn't a creak. The ladder stood as firm as if its legs had been riveted to the floor.

I experienced great satisfaction.

"With workmanship like this," I cried proudly, "the reconstruction of Italy is assured!"

Now it must be borne in mind that folding ladders, even brand-name ones, have one peculiarity: on one side are the rungs, and on the other are two lateral cross bars joined together at the base by another bar and fastened to the frame at the top by two bolts to guarantee the ladder's sure footing.

Being slightly absentminded, I took six steps up the one side but only one down (on the other side), a decisive step, and I crashed majestically to earth.

Albertino, who is cautious and shows a marked distaste for committing himself to anything, asked if I had fallen.

Margherita gazed fondly at me. "I feel you're closer to me now, Giovannino," she said in a far-away voice.

There was nothing but love in her words. But I must have answered with some irritation, for she held out her arms in perplexity.

"But how could you have hurt yourself," she said. "Isn't it a brand-name ladder?"

"Yes, it is. But when you fall from a ladder, brand names don't count—it's the law of gravity that counts."

Margherita shook her head. "Ah, then why do men struggle and strain and wear themselves out in a ceaseless search for improvement, for progress, reform, when only natural laws count? Didn't man a thousand years ago fall down ladders just as you did today?"

Up to now the Pasionaria had maintained a dignified restraint. She now planted herself firmly in front of Margherita, demanding peremptorily: "Why don't *you* try falling then, if you're so smart?"

TRAVELING IN ITALY

I know Margherita like the palm of my hand, so when we reached the first slope of the Futa pass I shifted gears and before she could say a word explained the situation to her.

"No, Margherita," I said, "the fact that though we're headed for Naples, we have to go up, not down, doesn't mean I've taken the wrong road. True, north is up and south is down, but that doesn't mean that when you head south you never have to go up and when you head north you never have to go down."

Ensconced in the back seat, Albertino was perusing his comic book, oblivious to the things of this world. Margherita turned her head for a moment to look at him tenderly.

"Don't ever tell him," she whispered in my ear. "He's a highly sensitive boy, and this would be a terrible disappointment. For him the south is always down. He still believes blindly in geography."

She remained lost in thought for a moment, then she sighed. "These days you can't believe in anything, not even the points of the compass."

When we got to Florence, I filled the car with gasoline and Albertino with comic books. I didn't have to fill the Pasionaria with anything. She had been left behind with a neighbor.

Then we sat down at a café.

"There," I said to Albertino, "is Giotto's *campanile*. If you want to look at it, there it is."

Albertino was reading his comic book.

"That the O?" he demanded, not raising his head.

"No," I said, "Giotto's O has nothing to do with Giotto's *campanile*. They are two absolutely different things."

"Okay," Albertino remarked, reading away.

We went to three cafés but couldn't find a waiter willing to acknowledge our existence, the place was so full of tourists. Finally at the fourth café a waiter deigned to take notice of us: he delivered a brief discourse in English.

"Two Campari sodas and an orangeade," I said in Italian, at which the waiter regarded us unfriendlily and took himself off in a rage.

"What a silly joke!" Margherita remarked. "You might have answered in English."

When I protested that I didn't speak English, Margherita declared that the study of foreign languages was the very stuff of life.

That's all I have to say about Florence.

We reached Rome toward evening, and suddenly, for Rome is a city that appears without warning. One turn of the road and there it was.

"The eternal city!" I cried, putting on the brakes.

I invited Albertino to look at Rome.

"Can you see the Colosseum?" Albertino inquired without interrupting his reading.

"Just a glimpse," I replied, "at the far end."

"Okay," Albertino assured me, "I can see it later, when it's nearer."

I turned to Margherita. "Rome!" I cried in a voice full of emotion. "Rome! Look at it!"

Margherita sighed heavily.

"Really, Giovannino," she said, "have you no delicacy at all? How can you expect a poor woman with her bones all but crushed from twelve hours in the car to even look at a city that size?"

I got annoyed. "But since that's Rome, that's all I can show you!"

"In that case, you should have the good grace to ignore it. Isn't it better to neglect Rome than to malign the mother of your children? You married me, didn't you, you didn't marry Rome."

I ignored Rome and got us there as fast as I could.

The next morning, having filled up with gasoline and comic books, we went to visit Saint Peter's.

We parked the car on this side of the famous colonnade and set off on foot, followed by Albertino, who was reading the latest Donald Duck. I mentioned that if he raised his head he could see the most famous church in the world.

"I know," he said. "It's the picture in my school reader."

Then I made use of my secret weapon. "But I bet that round thing there on the ground isn't in your school reader!"

Albertino raised his head and looked at the little marker I was pointing to on the pavement of the piazza near the obelisk. It did not, he admitted, appear in the photo in his school reader.

"In the picture there's a carriage there."

I took him to the left colonnade and had him observe

the four lines of columns. Then I led him to the famous little marker.

"Now look," I said. "How many rows of columns do you see?"

He had to admit he could see only one row of columns. Even Margherita looked, and cried out at the wonder of it. But Albertino controlled his emotion. He ran over to the colonnade, counted the columns, then turned to us.

"Four," he announced, "just as I thought. That round thing is a trick." And he returned to Donald Duck. "That's why they didn't put it in the school reader."

We wandered about till noon. Then Margherita expressed a desire to lunch in a typical Roman *osteria*. We passed about twenty but not until two in the afternoon did we come upon one that Margherita approved of. It was, Margherita said, a perfect example of a typical Roman *osteria*. Unfortunately, the sign read: *Trattoria Bolognese*.

After long study, Margherita decided what to order. They brought us three bowls of soup à la Pavese and three cutlets à la Milanese and a bottle of Bardolino wine. To compensate, the owner of the place was Tuscan and the waiter came from Genoa.

"We ought to send some picture postcards," Margherita said, after we had gone on to a café.

"Absolutely," I replied. "Some pretty views of Venice, saying 'Souvenir of Turin.'"

Margherita did not take offense: the Roman air had already exerted its charm over her. She sighed and in a faraway voice said: "What I'd like is to see all of Rome on foot—Rome dozing placidly in the spring sun. Is it far to the Boboli Gardens, Giovannino?"

"All the way back to Florence," I said as sweetly as I could. . . .

Albertino, meanwhile, continued studying his comic books. He neglected them only for a moment or two inside the Colosseum.

"I like this," he said at last. His verdict surely made the bones of the ancient Romans tremble with joy.

We reached Naples the following evening and Albertino, disillusioned when he learned that for the past four years Vesuvius hadn't even made a pretense of smoking, lost all interest in the city and its environs. When we got to Pompeii, I explained that it was a very old city buried in the ashes of an eruption of Vesuvius. Albertino, deep in his reading, sneered: he had lost all respect for volcanoes.

Two days later we were home, and we greeted the Pasionaria.

"She's been a very good girl," we were told by the woman who'd been looking after her.

The Pasionaria glared at us.

"But I'm not going to be good any more," she said. "I'm tired of being good. I need a rest."

And so ended our pleasure trip.

A BARGAIN

Suddenly one day we realized that our bicycles were poisoning our lives. For there were two of them, and they were always under foot, and it was too much trouble to put them away in the storeroom or the attic: maybe this was ungracious, but there has to be a limit even to ungraciousness.

Not only that, but the bicycles had already been claimed by Albertino and the Pasionaria, and every day they meticulously tried to climb up on the seats to see if their feet reached the pedals yet. A minor detail, no doubt, but actually of major import. Although they couldn't reach the pedals, the two scamps had no trouble at all reaching the doorbell and when we came to answer, they fell on us, bicycles and all.

Then one day Margherita and I found ourselves alone in the house. Albertino and the Pasionaria had been sent off to the mountains. And it was very strange: the house suddenly seemed as large as an empty barracks.

It was years since we had been alone in the house, and we looked at each other in astonishment.

"We're free!" cried Margherita.

We made a tour of the house, opening all the drawers and cupboard doors, examining every corner. And that's how we came on a jar of cherries preserved in brandy.

We ate all the cherries and then drank the brandy.

"Oh!" Margherita cried. "I feel a delicious warmth!"

I had a lot of work to do. My typewriter waited, frowning, its alphabet ready to march off, Indian file, into the world of fantasy. But "The hell with it!" I cried, slamming shut the canvas cover of the machine. And we went off to a bar.

I ate seven bags of salted almonds.

Margherita looked worried. "Giovannino," she said, "you know they'll make you sick."

"So what?" I replied. "The children aren't around, are they?"

We tiptoed home at two in the morning, furtively passing by the concierge's window.

"If she sees us," Margherita whispered, "and tells on us when those two get back, we'll be in trouble."

Fortunately we got home unobserved.

"We've put one over on the two mountaineers," Margherita crowed.

We sat in the kitchen and nibbled on peanuts and salted pumpkin seeds, reviewing with malice aforethought all Albertino's and the Pasionaria's faults. And this made us feel a little better: there was a lot to hold against those two.

It was hot, and Margherita went to open a window in Albertino and the Pasionaria's room to let in a little breeze. I heard a scream, and Margherita came rushing back in terror.

"There's a man in Carlotta's bed!"

Actually it was not a man but a bicycle, a woman's bicycle. The man's bicycle was in Albertino's bed.

Both had been carefully tucked in, each with a wheel on a pillow.

I found nothing remarkable in this, for I often came across a bicycle in the bathtub, soaking in the tepid water while the Pasionaria scrubbed the teeth of the gear with my toothbrush and my toothpaste.

A message from Albertino was pinned to the sheet: "Let them rest, they're tired of being up on their feet."

That was how Margherita and I realized that the bicycles were poisoning our lives. We decided to get rid of them.

"But the children have already claimed them," I said, on second thought.

"And how did we get the bicycles?" Margherita demanded. "Didn't we pay for them with the sweat of our brows?"

"With the sweat of my brow, Margherita."

"Mine or thine, what's the difference?"

We got the bicycles out of bed, and the next day a man came for them and left us a few coins in exchange.

We didn't haggle: this was not a question of money, this was a question of principle.

Several days passed, and then it was Saturday, and sunny, so we went off to the Porta Ticinese flea market. We browsed for a while among the junk. And then, in a place of honor, we came upon our bicycles, bright and shining in the sun, standing proudly on their stands, just as if they had been in a shop window.

We stopped to admire the bicycles, side by side, and when a man approached to examine them more closely, my heart began to beat very fast, and Margherita's must have beat fast too, because when the man, after a careful inspection, went off, Margherita sighed deeply.

"What a relief!" she cried.

Then a woman came. She circled Margherita's bicycle. "Hag!" murmured Margherita. And she sighed again when the woman asked the price of the bicyle, then tossed her head and made off.

"She's an idiot," Margherita announced. "A bicycle like that just isn't an ordinary old wreck."

We stayed quite a while, not right by the bicycles, but nearby, moving about slowly. Whenever we saw anyone take an interest, we came nearer.

The hours went by and the sun began to redden and still we waited.

"Maybe no one else will come," Margherita said. But at that very moment a horrible creature sauntered up and began to paw the seat of Margherita's bicycle. He tried out the handlebars, the steering, he tested the brakes; then, with one hoof on a pedal, he turned the wheel. Obviously he was a criminal of the worst sort, and Margherita watched him with terror. I had to resist an overwhelming urge to go smack his face.

The scoundrel left Margherita's bicycle and went over to haggle with the salesman. It looked as though they would never come to terms, when suddenly the ruffian pulled some money out of his pocket and threw it at the other man. Then he grabbed Margherita's bicycle and took off.

We watched in horrified silence: it was an intolerable insult. Once away from the crowd, the thief mounted the bicycle and pedaled off like the coward he was. Margherita stared, clutching my arm as though it was the oar that would save her in this shipwreck.

Now my bicycle stood alone amid the junk, clearly distressed in its solitary state. Margherita gazed sadly at it.

"When you were away," she said, "and I would feel low in the evening, I'd go to the place under the stairs where I'd hidden your bicycle, and I knew everything would work out all right. 'He's given me rides on that bicycle,' I would say to myself, 'and he's given Albertino rides. Of course he'll give the little girl rides on the bicycle too.' And then I felt better."

I made no reply. It's better to say nothing when a woman goes off like that. A man approached my lonely bicycle and began to fondle it. He must have liked it: after examining it minutely, he stepped back to take another look. But Margherita leaped in, grabbed the handlebars, and took the bicycle over to the salesman.

I saw her get some money out of her purse and thrust it into his hands. A moment later she was beside me, and between us stood my bicycle.

We walked for a bit with the bicycle between us, then I got on the seat, Margherita perched herself on the back, and off we went, as fast as we could go, ignoring the traffic policeman and oblivious to the car that waited for us in the parking lot.

As luck would have it, Margherita had paid for the one bicycle the precise amount we had received for the two bicycles. Yet we were in agreement: "It was a bargain."

And so I ask: is there a shred of logic in all of this?

There isn't. But what's the difference? You can go to the devil, you and your logic: I was pedaling my own bicycle, with Margherita beside me—a bedraggled couple, no doubt, on an old wreck of a bicycle, but to me it was a triumphal march.

THE OCTOBER REVOLUTION

The Pasionaria was ready to go out: she was sitting with quiet dignity in a corner of the sofa.

"Waiting," she said.

I got up, took my jacket, and put it on.

"I'm ready too," I said, heading for the door. But the Pasionaria didn't move, and when I reached the landing I turned and saw her still sitting serenely on the sofa.

"Well?" I said.

"Shave," said the Pasionaria in a quiet, even voice.

Now remember that I was born in the heart of the province of Emilia, a highly emotional part of the world, and that I am impulsive and prone to say things I hadn't intended to say. Faced by so presumptuous a demand, I reacted violently.

"When your mother met me I was unshaven, and when

she married me I was unshaven, and it's never entered her head that if I wanted to go out with her I had to shave. So who do you think you are?"

"I'm me," the Pasionaria answered in a calm, cool voice.

I shaved. Then I changed my jacket and brushed my shoes, and I did it all with such an air of superiority and distaste that the Pasionaria, if she didn't have the skin of a rhinoceros, would have understood how I felt.

We walked in silence through the streets in the mild Milanese autumn, and all too soon we arrived at our destination. There were people in the park in front of the school: mothers, fathers, little boys, little girls, school attendants. It was all like a scene from a movie. And I remembered the time before, when I brought Albertino to this same park and there abandoned him, and he melted into the herd like a brick into a wall.

In my hand I felt the warm little hand of the Pasionaria and I saw the mothers and children, and the fathers, but I wasn't feeling tender and sweet. There were harsh words in my mouth but I kept my mouth shut, I chewed the words and tried to swallow them, one by one, but many of them stuck in my throat. Once again I must bow to the tyranny and let go your hand, little girl, and watch you disappear into the hole in the wall.

Goodbye, Pasionaria, you're leaving my life, you're entering the life of the state. They'll teach you public hypocrisy, and even your thoughts will no longer be yours, and you'll begin to see with the eyes of the Minister of Education. Goodbye, goodbye.

Once again, as with Albertino, I must bow to the tyranny.

Leafing through old copies of the *Domenica del Cor-*

riere, I once smiled as I read about the women in the South who rebelled rather than have their children vaccinated. I didn't understand then, I thought only of the ignorance and superstition that had led those women to imagine the government doctors were some sort of sorcerers. But the women were acting on instinct. They thought they were defending their offspring from witchcraft, but in fact they were defending them from the tyranny of the state.

It's an essential tyranny, granted, but still the doctor's needle that inoculates your child with vaccine is a tentacle of the great monster, the state, goring a fresh young victim.

And I, who become indignant if the train—the train of state—is as much as five minutes late, am now bitterly unhappy because I must hand my daughter to the state to be taught the official ABC's.

Goodbye, Pasionaria.

The lines had formed, the mothers and fathers had withdrawn into the center of the park, and the children were now by themselves, single file against the school wall.

Only the Pasionaria was missing. I let go her fingers.

The doors opened. The children began to go in.

A taxi was at a corner. I ran to it, pulled open the door, threw myself in.

The car pulled away, racing through the streets of Milan on the way to the suburbs. In front of the blue waters of the port the taxi stopped and we got out.

I say "we" because the Pasionaria was with me. The Pasionaria was with the rebel.

The avenues bordering the lake were sun-drenched and empty and we had a very good time. But I knew that waiting for us at home was the state: Margherita. And this knowledge dampened my fun. And when we got back, at noon, Margherita asked the Pasionaria how it had gone, and the Pasionaria replied that it had gone very well, that the teacher was very nice, and so on and so on.

Then she looked at me and winked, in acknowledgment of our unspoken agreement that she was to say this and that. And so, with a wink, ended my October revolution.

THE GATE

The first really serious problem that raised its head in our new house was the gate.

The opening and shutting of a small iron gate, painted gray, would not seem in itself to be a complex operation: it was rendered complex by the fact that there was only one key. Anyone without a key had to ring and be let in—and let out.

Even if there had been two or three keys instead of one, of course, they could not have been entrusted to the children. One must never entrust house keys to children.

The problem was extremely serious because Albertino and the Pasionaria went to school at eight in the morning, and to get to school they had to leave the house, and to leave the house they had to use the gate. There was no domestic staff, so it was necessary for father or mother to get up out of bed at eight in the morning to open the gate. And given the case of a father who works at night and goes to bed at about five in the morning, and of a mother who is totally incapable of any kind of activity before 10 A.M., the problem rises to heights unknown.

The first morning I got up. The second morning Margherita got up. The third morning neither of us got up, and Albertino and the Pasionaria, somewhat disgruntled, remained at home.

That evening Margherita and I sat down to consider the situation. The idea of asking the two scholars to jump over the wall every morning was out. So was the suggestion of making a hole in the wall for them to pass through. (Others might pass through too, in the other direction. Might as well leave the gate wide open.)

Equip the gate with an automatic lock worked by a switch in the hall? But this would require the services of a mason, an electrician, a blacksmith—and a considerable outlay on the part of the head of the family.

It was then, unexpectedly, that the idea was born.

"Margherita," I said, "we are going too far in our search for truth. Truth is usually nearer than that, sometimes indeed within us. The thing is simplicity itself: the children open the gate, they pass through it, close it, giving two turns to the key, then they slip the key into the letter box inside the gate."

Although it was late in the day, we had an immediate

dress rehearsal. Albertino and the Pasionaria opened the gate, went out, locked it behind them, and dropped the key into the letter box. Then I took the key of the letter box, opened it, took out the key to the gate, and unlocked the gate. I went out, locked the gate, and dropped the key into the letter box.

"Magnificent!" cried Margherita. "Now I'm going to try it."

Margherita got the key, opened the gate, came out, locked the gate, then slipped the key through the slot of the letter box.

It was now late in the evening, and there we were, all four of us, out in the street. It was cold. I was in my robe and slippers, and so was Margherita. She looked at me perplexed.

"Giovannino, I don't know exactly what's wrong, something is."

"Well, the fact is," I said, "unless the cat opens the letter box, takes out the key to the gate and lets us in, we'll have to spend the night in the street. Moreover, we're going to be in exactly the same situation tomorrow morning."

When I mentioned a gate, did you think of the everyday kind, iron latticework put together more or less for art's sake? That's precisely the kind of gate we had. But my farsightedness had added a strong, thick wire netting to prevent ill-intentioned people from putting a hand through the bars to get at the lock or the letter box.

We persuaded Albertino to climb the wall, and as he was doing it, an elderly couple passing by observed loudly that only in this day and age do parents have the moral laxity to teach such tricks to their children.

"In my day," said the man, "fathers spanked children who tried to climb over walls and gates."

"And mothers," said the woman, "didn't parade through the streets at night in their robes."

With Albertino on the other side of the wall, there should have been no problem. Of course the letter box was locked. Margherita, after she had taken the gate key from the letter box, had closed and locked the box and put that key in her pocket. All she had to do now was pass the key to Albertino. Here, however, Margherita was guilty of a degree of thoughtlessness: she passed the key through— and dropped it in the slot of the letter box.

Even after I climbed over the wall, at no small sacrifice to my person, the incident was not yet closed: after me came Margherita, whose good fortune it was to have me to support her morally on one side of the wall and physically on the other. After she touched ground, there was the Pasionaria's voice from the street: "And me, who's going to get me over?"

So I made the dangerous journey again: back to the street, hand the Pasionaria over the wall to Margherita, climb over and down again. Three round trips in all.

Back in the house, we faced the problem of recovering the two keys. Margherita lightly suggested that we break the lock on the gate. It seemed simpler to me to unscrew the letter box and break *it* open. And so we did, and at midnight, order had been restored. Margherita drew a deep sigh.

"No, Margherita," I said, "this experience has been a useful one. It has revealed to us the hidden dangers in the system."

The next morning Albertino and the Pasionaria left at eight to go to school. They locked the gate behind them and put the key into the letter box. Albertino, however, put the key of the letter box in his pocket. When at ten I wanted to go out, I had to climb the wall again.

The delivery boys who supplied us with food threw the provisions over the wall. At eleven I had to climb the wall again to get back in. At noon Albertino and the Pasionaria returned and once more we had the key to the letter box and I was able to open the gate.

Margherita raged at the children.

"From now on," she said, "*I'm* going to keep the key to the letter box. We'll never get into a situation like *this* again!"

At three Margherita went out with the children (I was at work in my attic studio), locked the gate, and put the key in the letter box. At four I had a telephone call and had to hurry off to the Cathedral Square on important business. But Margherita had the key to the letter box, so I climbed over the wall.

At six Margherita returned alone, having left the children with Signora Marcella at Sempione, and found herself facing the locked gate—with the key to the gate inside the letter box. I came home at around eight. Margherita was walking up and down in front of the gate. Quite frankly, I didn't feel like climbing over the wall again. We ate at a restaurant and slept at a hotel.

The next day, a Sunday, we went out late in the afternoon to call for Albertino and the Pasionaria. Albertino climbed the wall, I handed him the key to the letter box and he opened the gate for us.

"This is a lunatic asylum," the Pasionaria observed, disgusted. "I'm sick of it."

Albertino and the Pasionaria now leave in the morning by way of the ground-floor window. But this can't go on. Something's going to have to be worked out.

THE EXAMINATION

I was sitting in front of the wide-open window, reading, when Albertino asked me: "Daddy, are you an honest man?"

Well, now, that isn't an easy question to answer.

"I don't know what business it is of yours," I grumbled.

"I need to know because I've got to write a theme about my parents—not like last year, height and width and circumference and so on, because this time it's about honesty and industry and activity and patriotism and all that."

Margherita interrupted.

"It appears to be a question of the parents' moral character," she said. "We think we lead a private life here within these walls, but the whole time the boy is keeping an eye on us."

"The girl too," declared the Pasionaria in a tone of gentle irony.

"This has nothing to do with you," Margherita retorted, annoyed. "We'll go into it with you when you're in the fourth grade, like your brother."

"Daddy, are you honest?" Albertino asked again.

"You must never ask that," I cried. "You know me, you know what I do, how I lead my life. You've got to decide for yourself whether I'm honest or not."

"Yes, but when I'm at school," Albertino said, "or when you're not in the house, how do I know what you do?"

"What magnificent confidence you have in your father!" I cried. "Do you think I behave like an honest man at home and like a crook outside?"

Margherita intervened. "That line of reasoning," she said, "isn't always reasonable. Plenty of people lead a double life. The boy's in no position to conduct an investigation into your private affairs. Come on, Giovannino, tell him, or he won't be able to write his essay."

"But he knows!" I shouted.

Albertino nodded, chewed his pen for a minute, then went over and whispered something in his mother's ear.

"Come on, Giovannino," Margherita said, "give him an answer."

"I," I said, "am a man of honor, and I fail to see how there could be any doubts on the subject."

Once again Albertino nodded, then went over to whisper to his mother again.

"Yes, of course," I heard her say, "a man of honor and an honest man are the same thing."

Albertino wrote something in his notebook.

Five minutes passed in silence. Then Albertino returned, more cautiously, to the attack: "Daddy, are you industrious too?"

"Yes, Albertino," I replied, "I am industrious, I love my work, I make all kinds of sacrifices for the sake of my family, my country, and civilization."

Albertino carefully copied my words down in his notebook, then raised his head: "And what kind of father are you?"

I refused to reply.

"That," I declared, "you must judge for yourself. You're my child."

"I'm your child too!" cried the Pasionaria.

"Certainly you are," I said, "and it's you, my children, who must say what kind of father I am."

Albertino and the Pasionaria retired to the next room, presumably to come to an agreement concerning my qualities as a father. The discussion was long and animated. Finally Albertino returned, went to his desk, and resumed his writing. I glanced over at him, but his expression was impenetrable.

I looked at the Pasionaria. She winked.

The Pasionaria knows how to protect herself against the dangers of literacy. When Albertino finished writing, she took his notebook over to Margherita. They consulted together and then Margherita glanced at the page and reassured the Pasionaria: it was all right.

Albertino blotted the page and put the notebook into his satchel. His sister congratulated him. Margherita murmured in my ear: "A bit harsh perhaps, but on the whole sympathetic."

I breathed a sigh of relief. I had passed my examination.

THE THOUSAND-LIRE STORY

I went down to the center of town to make some purchases, and in the end found myself without cigarettes and with a single thousand-lire note in my wallet.

I went into a tobacconist's, asked for a package of Swiss cigarettes, and laid the thousand-lire note on the counter.

The tobacconist looked at it with interest. "What is it?" he asked.

"A thousand-lire note," I replied.

The tobacconist called to his wife, who was reading a newspaper at the other end of the counter.

"Maria, look at this!"

The woman turned her head and without bothering to come nearer glanced at the note.

"Ah," she said, "it's back in the center of town again."

The tobacconist asked if I lived at Porta Volta.

"Lambrate," I said.

"Then it's moved around," he remarked. "It hasn't been here in about a month. We all know it."

I looked at the note again and caught my breath. It was the falsest thousand-lire note in the world, so shamelessly counterfeit as to inspire the liveliest disgust.

There ought to be a certain amount of care, professional pride, taken in the production even of counterfeit thousand-lire notes. But the note I had in front of me was no more than a free and arbitrary interpretation of a real thousand-lire note.

I handed back the cigarettes and picked up the offending note.

"Too bad!" cried the tobacconist. "But in this life you've got to learn to take the knocks philosophically."

I started off for the parking lot but of course had to give up the idea of reclaiming my car—or of taking a taxi, or even a bus. I arrived home on foot, in an unenviable state of mind.

"Everything go all right?" Margherita asked me.

"Fine," I replied, ashamed to admit I'd accepted the counterfeit thousand-lire note.

"Oh, good!" Margherita cried. "You were able to get rid of that awful counterfeit note I put in your wallet."

I am not speaking here to children, I'm speaking to grown men, to old hands at matrimony. They'll understand: they know that the ladies play these little tricks.

I maintained my composure. I took the note from my pocket and handed it to Margherita.

"If you're simple-minded enough to accept such a horror," I said, "you ought to be honest enough to face up to it. Take that thousand-lire note and burn it. Furthermore, it's a crime to circulate counterfeit bills. Look, it's down right here, on the note itself, in this little box. Read it."

"Whoever gave it to me," she said, "ought to take it back."

"Who gave it to you, Margherita?"

"I don't know. I shop all over the neighborhood, anybody might have given it to me."

She went out and was back after a couple of hours, so she must have worked fast. To quarrel with the bakery, the grocery, the drug store, the fruit shop, the butcher, the dry goods store, and the tobacco shop takes a bit of time. However, when Margherita returned she still had the counterfeit thousand-lire note.

The concierge, in matters of this nature, is invaluable. Margherita called her and handed the whole thing over to her.

"If you can get rid of it," Margherita said, "we split."

Two days passed; and then the concierge came back and handed Margherita a perfectly good five-hundred-lire note.

"I had to take it out of the neighborhood," the concierge explained. "Everybody here knows that bill by heart. Now let it go where it will."

Then one day the concierge came running up.

"It's come back!" she cried. "An old woman tried to pass it to the grocer!"

In the following days, the wretched thing was seen by the druggist, the butcher, the fruit seller, and the stationer, and the general apprehension increased. Then it wasn't mentioned any more—quite simply because Margherita had it in her purse.

When we found it, we looked at it in horror—which I cut short: I took the infamous note and was about to feed it to the stove. But Margherita grabbed it from me.

"It's a matter of principle," she said. "I took it, I have to get rid of it."

The days that followed were sad ones for all the family. Margherita ventured into far-distant neighborhoods and returned every night dead tired. At last she had to give up. She called the concierge and once more entrusted the note to her, under the same conditions as before.

The neighborhood resumed its state of siege, for the concierge went into action at once, unleashing all the housemaids who came to see her. Then there was peace. She reappeared after a week and handed to Margherita a glorious five-hundred-lire note.

"I got away with it," she said. "But I had to go all the way to Baggio. Now that it's out in the suburbs, we can all relax."

Margherita, who has her own conception of arithmetic, was particularly content that evening.

"Giovannino," she said, "we're even now. I got five hundred lire the first time, and five hundred lire the second time. A thousand lire went out and a thousand lire came back."

I made no objection to this statement but I went to bed in a guilty frame of mind. At one in the morning, Margherita woke with a start.

"Giovannino!" she cried. "If I get that counterfeit bill back and make the same deal with the concierge, I'll make a profit of five hundred lire."

"Don't think about it," I said.

Four weeks passed. Then one evening I heard a shriek and I ran to the kitchen. There was Margherita, staring wide-eyed into a cabinet drawer. Inside it was the counterfeit thousand-lire note.

This time I didn't hesitate. I picked up the note and took it over to the gas stove. Margherita made no objection. But before the bill touched the flame, the gas went out.

At this, a terrible moan came from Margherita, and she sank into a chair.

Of course it was chance. A reasonable man would laugh

and light a match and touch it to the bill. But I did not. I put the thousand-lire note back in the drawer. Every once in a while Margherita and I would peek in, and there it was always, evil and obstinate, and so false you could tell it even with the drawer shut.

One day I told the story to a friend of mine who works in a bank, and he said he'd like to see the note. We took it to him.

Margherita shuddered as she saw the ease with which he handled the bill, and felt it, and held it to the light.

"There are defects in the printing," he said finally, "but the bill is not counterfeit."

He put it with some others and gave us two five-hundred-lire notes.

In the street, Margherita paused and said: "Giovannino, I got five hundred lire from the concierge the first time, and I got five hundred the second time, and just now we got a thousand. That makes two thousand lire. We've made a thousand lire clear! Is it possible?"

"Anything is possible," I said, "but if you ask me, we have paid the wages of sin."

THE LADY AND THE "E"

The Pasionaria is struggling with "e," and the struggle is titanic. For one thing, her notebook paper is poor stuff and keeps wrinkling up like the face of a laughing octogenarian. For another, her pen has a nasty point that keeps sticking through the paper. And her ink, in addition, has only to glimpse a patch of white to begin to spread like a black cloud.

Then too, besides the fact that "e" is a cowardly opponent and capricious as well, it must be borne in mind that the Pasionaria began school unencumbered by cultural paraphernalia. Last summer someone put a pencil in her hand and a notebook in front of her and tried to persuade her to copy some lines—but she did not lose her head. She laid the pencil down on the desk and closed the notebook.

"I can already read the lines," she said. "And when I go to school, I'll learn how to write them."

And now she's struggling with "e," and the struggle is titanic.

When she reached the fifth "e," she paused to recover her breath. Margherita was stretched out on the sofa, asleep. The Pasionaria gazed at her for a moment and sighed.

"While I work," she said, "she sleeps."

"But she," I said, "already knows how to write 'e.' "

"You do too," replied the Pasionaria, "but you're not sleeping."

"A question of temperament."

"And you help me sometimes," the Pasionaria went on. "You fix my toys when they break, and all that. But what does she do for me? . . . Sometimes," she sighed, "I could just die."

I felt anxious.

"How many times?" I asked.

She raised three ink-stained fingers.

"Oh." And I handed her a couple of caramels, which she began to chew.

She returned to her task with a will, took up her pen, dipped it in ink, and bent over her notebook. But the pen got stuck in the paper, then skimmed over to bury itself in the wood of the desk.

"Stay there," she cried, "lord and master!" And she turned to me.

"What good is it?" she demanded furiously.

"What good is what?"

" 'E.' "

"It's essential. We'd be lost without 'e.' Could you say 'sheep,' for instance, without 'e'?"

"I *know* how to say it. It's the writing that's hard. They could make it less complicated at least. I like 'i'!"

I told her "e" was the basis of everything. And she took up her pen again, but before returning to the struggle, experienced one more bout of rebelliousness.

"And meanwhile *she*," the Pasionaria cried, "she goes right on sleeping!"

"We could exchange her," I said, "perhaps get one that's younger and nicer."

The Pasionaria had resumed her life-and-death struggle with the hostile "e." With a shrug of her shoulders, she murmured: "For the time being let's hold on to her. But one of these days, you'll see, something awful's going to happen!"

THE STRANGER

There comes a moment in every family when Papa realizes he's got a stranger in the house. It happened to me, I recall, at the table. I sat there and reviewed my family carefully, one by one, and we were still four: Margherita, Albertino, the Pasionaria, and Giovannino. Yet I felt there was a stranger there, and he was sitting right across from me. He was Albertino.

Although Albertino was only nine at the time, he had undertaken the control of his own affairs, all by himself. He was extremely dignified and rather reserved, and in his daily reports to me he limited himself to the communication of only the most essential information. In the course of a week during which I found him more than usually loquacious, I heard his voice maybe three times. On Monday morning he came to my workroom to tell me the coffee was ready. Thursday evening after supper he raised his head from the book he was reading and asked me who the antipodes were. Saturday he and his mother went away for the weekend, and before departing he said goodbye to me.

He asks me for help only in cases of extreme need. One day he told me his teacher wanted him to take a piece of paper a meter square and divide it into squares of ten centimeters, and then divide one of the ten-centimeter squares into one-centimeter squares.

I have seldom worked so carefully or with such precision. I took a large sheet of paper and on it I drew a one-meter square, within the square I drew the ten-centimeter lines, and finally, in the first small square in the upper right-hand corner, I made the one-centimeter divisions.

"Is that all right?" I asked when I was finished.

Albertino measured the sides of the large square to make sure each was exactly one meter; then he counted, one by one, the ten-centimeter squares; and then he counted, one by one, the one-centimeter squares.

"One square centimeter is missing," he said at last. "There are only ninety-nine."

I said that was impossible.

"Each side of the square," I told him, "is divided into ten equal parts, and the parallel lines, if you admit that ten times ten make a hundred, must form exactly one hundred equal squares. Count them again and you'll see."

"That isn't necessary," Albertino replied. "I trust you."

This gave me great pleasure, but there is no need to go on about it, that's the kind of boy Albertino is. And then one evening I realized that there was a stranger in my house and the stranger was Albertino.

I said nothing to Margherita. If anyone were to speak to Margherita about strangers in the house, there would ensue a dramatic scene fit for a detective mystery. I stretched out on the couch in my workroom and waited.

Sure enough, after a little while, Albertino came in.

"One of the boys in school," Albertino announced, "told me you write books."

I said I had indeed written some books.

"I'd like to read them," said Albertino.

There it was, and it was quite unexpected. I was taken by surprise and felt as if I'd been found out in something less than respectable.

"They're all there," I said, "in a row on the second shelf of the bookcase." I tried to be calm.

Albertino looked through the books on the shelf, and I examined my conscience. No, I decided, I needn't worry: not even in my first books was there anything that might be harmful to a nine-year-old boy.

"May I take this one?"

It was my last collection of stories, and I said yes, of course.

When later I passed by the door of his room, he was reading.

I told Margherita.

"He asked to read one of my books," I said.

"Someone must have told him you write," Margherita said. "That's one of the troubles with public schools. Younger children come together with the older ones and pick up things they shouldn't."

Margherita, you see, believes that my profession,

though in essence an honest one, isn't very serious. From time to time she brings up the fact that I did not take a degree. "If you had a degree, Giovannino," she says, "and a decent job, you could still write if you wanted to."

She sighed. "You shouldn't have given it to him," she said. "You've made a mistake."

I got angry and said there wasn't anything shocking or bad in my book.

"But you wrote it, Giovannino. Children should never read books their fathers have written. If it was scientific stuff, chemistry or physics or something like that, then all right, but literary stuff, absolutely not. And particularly what you write—one can never tell when you're joking and when you're not, or whether you're inventing things or telling the truth. Who knows how he'll take it?"

"Let him take it as he likes!" I cried. "A lot of people read my books and find them all right. Even in other countries there are people who like my books."

I turned out the light, but my brain paid no heed.

I saw Albertino at lunch the next day and looked as disinterested as I knew how. Albertino took no part in the family discussion. The same thing happened that evening. The following evening, however, I was napping on the couch in my workroom, when Albertino appeared.

He had my book in his hands. He went to the bookcase, replaced the volume in the second shelf, then turned to go.

"Did you read it?" I asked.

"Oh, yes," he answered. "It's written in big letters and goes fast."

That was all he said.

PRISONER OF DREAMS

When they reach a certain age, women begin to make important discoveries.

"Giovannino," Margherita said to me one day, "has it ever occurred to you that I have within me a world that is entirely mine?"

"No, Margherita," I said.

"I have a world that's all mine within me," Margherita explained. "Oh yes, I live in our everyday external world, but I also live in a secret world all my own. I move alone, sad, hopelessly alone through the streets of that world. And sometimes I get lost and frightened and cry out for help—but no one hears me."

A problem.

"If the world's all your own," I said, "you must know it pretty well."

"It's a world that belongs to me," said Margherita, "only in the sense that I belong to it. I am a prisoner of that world of shadows, desires, and fears—a prisoner, and alone. And I drag my unhappy feet through streets that never end."

"A bad business," I said. "Couldn't you at least get hold of a bicycle?"

Margherita looked at me with disgust.

But I went on. "I'm not joking, Margherita. I'm only

trying to help you. Since it's a world that's entirely yours, where you live in your thoughts, you can concentrate on traveling on a bicycle instead of on foot, and you'd feel much better, believe me. I'd have said a car, but you don't drive."

A few days later she spoke of her world again, and I asked: "Margherita, did you try thinking what I told you?"

"Yes."

"And did you manage to get hold of a bicycle?"

"Yes," she said. "It wasn't easy. That world is a poetic world. But finally, through sheer force of will, I won out."

"Is it better, traveling around on a bicycle?"

"Well, I am less tired and I can do a great many more streets."

For a week Margherita was in high spirits. Evidently, not having to travel on foot had been of considerable benefit to her. Then one day she fell into a deep depression.

"Margherita," I said, "how are things in that world of yours?"

She sighed. "Not well."

"How about the bicycle?"

"I've had to go back to walking. I had a blow-out."

I lost my head.

"Margherita," I cried, "if you managed to get hold of a bicycle, you ought to be able to fix the tire by thinking of a bit of rubber, a tube of cement, and a bicycle pump."

"I have all of that, and I've tried. But I can't get it fixed."

"It's so easy, Margherita! Try again!"

She shook her head.

"Isn't there a bicycle shop in that world of yours?"

"In that world of mine there are only shadows, desires, fears. It's terrible, Giovannino, I'm so alone there!"

I took her hand and led her to the large room that serves as both garage and workshop. I took down my bicycle from the wall and showed her how easy it was to change a tire. I even had her try it. And after several attempts, she succeeded.

Then I left her to her thoughts. She seemed more cheerful.

I gave her three days. Then I asked her point-blank: "Well? Everything okay?"

"I can't do it, Giovannino," she replied. "It must be a different kind of tire. And just look what it's done to my hands."

She held them out. They were soft and unblemished. She was showing me the hands of her mind, and I admitted that they were somewhat battered.

"Don't give up hope, Margherita. I'm here to help you," I said.

"But you're not there. There I'm alone with a bicycle I can't use."

We went back to the garage and I had her change the tire of my bicycle again and again. Recalling the instructions given with a machine gun, I had her repeat the operation blindfolded.

For the next two days she seemed preoccupied, and I knew she was struggling with that tire. The third day she was triumphant.

"I made it!" she cried. "The bicycle is fixed and works perfectly."

Weeks passed, and months, before Margherita spoke

again of her secret world. We were alone in the house one evening, and Margherita looked at me with tears in her eyes.

"What's happened, Margherita? What is it?"

"I fell, Giovannino. I was riding along a narrow mountain road in my world and the bicycle slipped out from under me. I rolled all the way down."

She covered her face with her hands.

"And where are you now, Margherita?"

"At the bottom of a ravine," she sobbed.

"Hurt?"

"Hurt."

"Badly?"

"It can't be so very bad. I can move. It's only my head that hurts."

"Have you tried calling for help?"

But of course it was useless to call for help in a world of shadows, desires, and fears. I told her to get hold of herself and rest a bit before trying to climb out.

A couple of days later, Margherita told me she no longer felt any pain in her head, but trying to get out of the gorge was hopeless.

"It's the end," she sobbed, "unless someone throws a rope down to me. I'm devoured by thirst."

I went to the bookstore and bought all the manuals they had on mountain climbing. Margherita and I studied the illustrations. We found the type of rock formation within whose walls Margherita was imprisoned. We read the manual, and she learned by heart the movements I thought would be of use to her.

For three days Margherita tried to climb that steep mountain wall. The fourth she showed me her hands:

they were smooth and white, but I could see how scratched and bloody they were.

"I'm done in," Margherita said. "I feel the end approaching. Soon there'll be nothing but a heap of bones at the bottom of the ravine."

I cursed the bicycle and cried that I was to blame for the whole thing.

"No," Margherita said, "it's fate. I'd have fallen even without the bicycle. We must be resigned."

But I didn't want her to be resigned.

"Cry out!" I said. "Cry out with all the strength you've got left. Cry out."

"It's no use, Giovannino. There's nobody there."

"Cry out, cry out day and night. Try to call me. Don't stop calling me. Who knows, I may hear you."

I went to the garage and kicked my bicycle. Then I kicked the motorcycle too and hurt my foot, and I had a very disagreeable day. In the evening the sky was ugly and full of dark clouds and threats of distant thunder. It began to rain, but I stayed by the sea, where I had spent the afternoon. After the storm ended, the world was silent and dark. And I heard a distant cry: "Giovannino!"

I got on my motorcycle and sped toward the city. At home, Margherita was humming as she set the table.

"Margherita, did you call?"

"I called and called. And at last you heard me. I saw you leaning over the ravine."

"Did I have a rope with me?"

"Yes, you had a long rope."

"Thank God!"

"You had a long rope and you threw it down to me. I tied myself to it and you pulled me up."

"Hurray!" I cried, and praised God for having created mountain-climbing manuals.

"It was marvelous," Margherita sighed. "The minute I got up on safe ground again, you kicked the bicycle down into the ravine."

I took pride in my feat of strength.

"Then what did I do?" I asked.

"You went away."

"I'm sorry about that. It was a terrible thing to leave you alone in that horrible, dangerous world. And without even a bicycle."

But Margherita was perfectly serene.

"Only shadows, desires, and fears live in my secret world. But I'm not worried any more. I know that if I'm ever in danger and I call to you, you'll hear me and come."

THE CHAUFFEUR

"Here," said the Pasionaria, "in this lousy house—"

I interrupted: " 'Lousy' is a vulgar word, unsuitable to well-brought-up people."

"I'm not well brought up," the Pasionaria declared. "I have parents who always need a shave, and their pants are always covered with paint and oil, and they get up at eleven even if their children have to go to school at eight, and they are always saying that when they were my age they knew how to do this and how to do that and the other . . ."

Unperturbed, I continued oiling my car.

She sighed.

"In this lousy house," she said, "everybody's married except me."

"Everybody?"

"Everybody," the Pasionaria repeated firmly. "You're married to your wife, your wife is married to her husband, my grandmother is married to your father, my grandfather is married to your mother. Even the woman who comes to do the laundry is married to her husband. Why, even the pigeons are married! But not me."

I asked her to take note of the fact that her brother, although he was almost four years older than she, was still a bachelor, and didn't complain about it.

She shrugged her shoulders.

"Yes, he's a bachelor," she said, "but when he's grown up, he'll have a job. I'm a bachelor too, but when I'm grown up I won't be able to do anything because I weighed only three and a half pounds when I was born and I have small bones."

She leaned over and tried to lift a piece of brick which could not have weighed more than twelve ounces. Even with both hands, she succeeded only in budging it slightly.

"See how weak I am?" she said. "And now my back's bothering me. The slightest effort, and I get nervous exhaustion. But I don't stay in bed till eleven like that woman."

The Pasionaria, it is true, weighed only a little over three and a half pounds at birth. And she does have small bones and is tiny. But still, the big act she put on—of being unable to lift a bit of brick weighing twelve ounces —was not to be tolerated.

"Six and a half," I observed, "is rather young to be worried about getting married. You'll get married when the time comes—if you can find a husband."

"And if I can't?"

"Oh, you can always find a husband, all you have to do is look."

"Me, I'm not like some women, I don't go looking for husbands. I'm not a woman who has nothing but a handkerchief and a toothbrush."

The allusion was to Margherita: ours was not a marriage of money and interest. Margherita's dowry did consist of a handkerchief and a toothbrush—albeit charming and of excellent quality. This did not, however, excuse the sarcasm in the Pasionaria's voice.

"Dowries," I affirmed, "aren't worth a fig. As you have pointed out, your mother found a husband though she possessed nothing but a handkerchief and a toothbrush."

The Pasionaria sighed. "Yet she's always saying, poor woman, that she'd be better off if she hadn't married."

I gave the Pasionaria a belligerent look, but she didn't flinch.

"Me," she said, "I want a clean, well-dressed husband who doesn't holler like a madman and who brings flowers home and says, 'Darling, these are for you,' like Signor

Luigi, though of course his wife had a dowry and I know she did because she's always saying so to your wife and then she shows her all the linen and the clothes and the sterling silver and the box with the gold stuff inside and so on and so on."

The Pasionaria sat down on a step.

"What I need now," she said, in a disheartened tone, "is a bit of sea air. But how am I going to get it? This everlasting dependence! Well, there's nothing to do about it. But the day I really take to my bed, that'll be a day."

I paused in my work.

"Instead of eavesdropping on your mother," I said, "I suggest you read one of your magazines."

"Nothing amuses me any more," sighed the Pasionaria. "And then, you know, even for magazines, even for candy, for *everything*, it's always a question of depending on someone else."

To put an end to this unsettling conversation, I reached into my pocket and handed all my loose change to the Pasionaria. The money was accepted as partial payment on the dowry, and the Pasionaria cheered up.

I continued my work in peace. After a while I heard a ring at the gate and then saw a blond little girl, splendidly dressed. The Pasionaria did the honors of the house.

As they came within earshot, I heard the Pasionaria's voice: "This is our car. It's dirty now but when it's clean it's beautiful."

"And is that your father?" the little blonde whispered.

"No, Papa's out," the Pasionaria replied. "That's our chauffeur."

"We have a chauffeur too," said the little blonde. "But

he wears a uniform with lots of buttons and a cap with a visor. He's very good."

"Ours is better," the Pasionaria replied. "He won a medal in Paris."

The little blonde was much impressed and looked at me with considerable respect.

"A gold medal as big as that!" the Pasionaria added, and the little blonde opened her eyes wide.

As a father I felt somewhat deflated, but I took great pride in my position as chauffeur.

When the visit ended, the Pasionaria came to me.

"My friend has to be driven home," she said competently, and I replied, as competently, that I wouldn't dream of it. But my chauffeur's pride won out. I washed my hands, brushed my clothes, put on a jacket, and brought the car around to the front of the house.

"I do hope you'll call on me again when you have the time," said the Pasionaria as the little blonde got into the car.

I closed the door after her.

"Put up a good show for me," the Pasionaria whispered.

During the drive, the little blonde addressed me. "Is it true you won a gold medal in Paris?"

"Yes, a big medal."

She asked me what Paris was like, and I replied at length, and to her complete satisfaction.

When we arrived, I got out and opened the door for her.

"Wait a minute," she said, and she ran into the house.

She returned with a slice of cake and an enormous apple.

"I think your employers," said the little blonde, "aren't very nice people and they probably don't give you enough to eat."

I thanked her and left.

Back home there was trouble. The Pasionaria laid claim to half the slice of cake.

"If it hadn't been for me," she declared, "she wouldn't have given you the tip."

WRITINGS ON THE WALL

When you draw up a contract, you've got to be quite precise, specifying every detail. Otherwise, before you're done, you're in for some unpleasant surprises.

The Pasionaria pledged herself, in my presence, to behave in a specified manner for a specified length of time. I pledged myself, in her presence, to give her an all too vaguely defined "nice present," the precise nature of which was to be agreed upon by mutual consent. The Pasionaria fulfilled her part of the contract, and I declared myself ready to do my part. I asked her to say what she wanted. And she announced with the utmost clarity: "I want to write on the wall with a white brush."

I am a champion of liberty both in public and at home. In my house I'm in charge, but the others make the decisions, because I count for one and the other three have a clear majority. I did not cry, "No!" to the Pasionaria's request. I merely tried to achieve an honorable compromise. I would supply a can of white paint, a brush, and paper or board on which to write.

Writing on walls is, I feel, a kind of sabotage of the reconstruction effort. The Republic protects the national landscape, and the family is duty-bound to protect the domestic landscape.

"I want to write on the wall," the Pasionaria repeated. The Pasionaria is only six and a half but she is already a person in her own right. She has character, dignity, ideas —small ideas, perhaps, but extraordinarily clear.

Still hoping to find a suitable compromise, I offered the walls of the cellar.

"I want to write with a white brush," the Pasionaria affirmed, "on the outside wall, not on an inside wall."

If the paint were sufficiently diluted, I decided, and the writing washed off while it was still fresh, no great damage would be done to our walls. I felt more cheerful.

"I want to write on the outside wall," the Pasionaria went on, "on the outside wall in the street. I don't like it here, this wall's mine."

A father must never forget his duties as an educator. I explained that to daub the walls of others is a twofold offense, both against private property and against public order.

"Lots of walls are covered with big letters," she said.

If in the end I gave in, my surrender may be accounted for by the simple fact that the Pasionaria is my daughter.

I filled a can with white paint, well thinned, got hold of a good brush, and off we went in the car.

"When I see the wall I like, I'll tell you," the Pasionaria announced.

We did quite a bit of driving before we found a place that fulfilled the necessary conditions. It was on the far edge of the city: the long encircling wall of a small country house, isolated and abandoned.

We got out of the car.

"You watch if anyone comes," said the Pasionaria. "If you see anyone, whistle."

"Have you got a lot to write?"

"I don't know, I haven't decided," she whispered.

"Well, try to hurry. If the police catch us, we'll both go to jail."

"You, too?"

"Of course."

She stared at the brush and the can of white paint. Then she brightened.

"Don't worry," she said. "If they catch me, I won't say you're my papa."

"That wouldn't do any good. You'd have to tell them your name, and they'd come to the house and arrest me."

She looked at me. "What about all the other people who have written on walls? Have they arrested all of them?"

I had to say I didn't know. In any case, our situation was complicated because when they arrest a child they take the parents too.

"That woman too?" the Pasionaria asked, annoyed.

"Well, of course. Parents are father and mother both."

"She's always meddling in my affairs!" cried the Pasionaria. "Whatever I do, out she pops. Now I can't even do my writing because she's afraid of her own shadow and if the police come to the house she'll faint."

The Pasionaria dipped the brush into the can and stood watching the white paint drip down. "If a person can't do anything," she cried, "it's always on account of the wife!"

I made no comment. I've said the same thing several thousand times.

"Well," sighed the Pasionaria, "nothing to do. Let's go home."

"No," I said, "write all you want."

She started to protest, but I cut her short.

"I order you to write anything you want. If the police come, it's my fault, I ordered it, I'm the one who's responsible. Anyway, I'm not afraid of the police—I've had lots of experience in these matters, I was a prisoner for a long time."

This impressed the Pasionaria.

"Then they won't take *her* too?" she asked.

"What's she got to do with it? I'm the one who told you to do it. Go ahead, *write!*"

The Pasionaria looked at me. "Can I write 'Viva Coppi'?"

My house enjoys total freedom of the press. I told her she could write what she wanted. Certainly Coppi was a great man.

It is now that I wish I were one of those self-educated people who haven't been spoiled by the grammar and syntax taught in school and who therefore can write wonders. But I, rather than spoil the picture, will not attempt to describe the Pasionaria as she worked on the wall of the lonely, abandoned house. She was evidently deeply preoccupied with her work, for she forgot a detail of some importance: that Coppi is spelled *Coppi* and not *Copi*.

Out of a certain delicacy, I did not tell her.

A fellow appeared in the far distance, on a bicycle, and I whistled. We fled to the car, leaving the brush on the ground. But the man turned off a hundred yards or so before he reached us, and the Pasionaria was able to perfect her writing with the major addition of an underscore.

"If *you* want to write now," said the Pasionaria, "I'll keep watch. But I can't whistle. If someone comes, I'll say, 'Bowwow!'"

I agreed, and while the Pasionaria watched, I wrote, "Viva Girardengo."

The Pasionaria barked. I threw down the brush and we fled once again into the car. Some local authority was approaching on a bicycle. I threw the car into gear and we were off.

"Just in time," I said, when we were out of range.

The Pasionaria wanted to know who Girardengo was, and I said he was Coppi's father.

"Who's Bartali's father?" she asked.

"Bartali?" I cried indignantly. "I don't want to hear his name mentioned!"

She spoke no more of him.

On a wall in the Viale Romagna we saw, written in letters a yard high, "CROOK SCELBA."

"Does he race too?" asked the Pasionaria.

"No, he doesn't race. He tries to make other people race."

Before turning the last corner, we stopped at a café and I ordered two ice creams.

"Not for me," said the Pasionaria. "I don't want it, I don't like that junk. If I were your wife, I wouldn't let you eat it either."

I sighed—perhaps over the irresponsibility of the modern wife.

COLLABORATION

Every once in a while my inspiration runs dry. I feel as though my head is full of air. I write a line, I pull the page out of the typewriter, I throw it away. I put in another sheet, I light another cigarette. But in which cigarette does inspiration lie? The fifteenth? The twenty-fifth?

For three hours I had been looking for a hook to hang a few words on. Every now and then I thought I'd found it, and I put a line down, but after the words were on the paper I'd take it out of the machine.

The Pasionaria came in with a cup of coffee for me.

Inspiration may also be found in a cup of coffee. But in which? The fourth? The seventh?

The Pasionaria looked at me.

"No good," I said.

"Drink your coffee now," she said gravely. "Then it'll be good."

She sat down across from me and looked at me in silence. I drank the coffee, but there was no inspiration in that cup either.

"Still no good," I said.

She came over to me.

"Try this," she said, handing me a piece of candy. "It's lemon."

I chewed the piece of lemon candy, but it didn't have any ideas in it either.

She left me, and returned shortly with Margherita.

"Still nothing?" she asked.

Disconsolately, I shook my head.

"You're weak, that's the trouble," Margherita declared. "When a person is weak, he can't do anything. If a car has no gasoline, it won't run, will it?"

The two left and came back after a bit, accompanied by Albertino and bearing food and drink. I ate and drank, but not a single idea came to me.

They watched me for a time in silence, then Margherita said: "I think sometimes any old suggestion will do the trick—it gives you a starting point. Why don't you try writing an adventure story?"

That was certainly an idea. But I still needed a story idea.

Margherita took cognizance of the fact and thought hard for a while.

"All right," she said at last. "Once I read a charming story—"

"If you read it," I broke in, "that means somebody wrote it. There's no point in my writing it again."

Margherita shook her head.

"One must admit," she sighed, "you've got a hard job. But that's no reason to be discouraged. You do your own thinking, and meanwhile we'll try to work something out."

The three of them left me, and from the other room I could hear a long, whispered discussion.

"Now then," said Margherita, returning with her troupe, "if you were to write the story of two—"

"Three," the Pasionaria corrected her. "There's the one with the car."

"Right!" said Margherita. "And I think it's a good idea. These three people want to go on a trip—"

"Two," Albertino corrected her. "One has to stay at home to wait for a telephone call."

"Right!" cried Margherita. "All right then, this is how it is: there are three people, but only two of them go away, because one stays home—he's waiting for a telephone call."

I asked who the three were.

"Three friends," Margherita answered. "Three young men."

The Pasionaria shook her head. "No," she said, "first there were three boys, then we decided it was two men and a girl."

Margherita looked uncertain.

"Two men and a girl?" she said. "What's that girl doing with two men?"

"With one," Albertino amended. "The other one's at home waiting for the telephone call."

It wasn't such a bad idea. But it needed figuring out. Who was the man waiting for the phone call, who was the girl, who was the other man?

Margherita had a whispered discussion with Albertino and the Pasionaria. Then she communicated the result to me.

"He's in business, the one who's waiting for the telephone call. Now the other one, we don't know what he does exactly. As for the girl, it seems she's the daughter of a man who lives in the same building. At this point," said Margherita, "the story gets a little complicated—"

Albertino tried to simplify it. "The friend of the one who's waiting for the telephone call goes out and he meets her coming downstairs so they say hello and they go out together. That's clear."

"Yes, it's clear enough," Margherita admitted. "The action takes place without a lot of difficulties. But I can't figure out what the one who stays at home is doing."

"Waiting for the telephone call!" cried the Pasionaria.

"Yes, but who from?"

"After they phone, he knows. Meanwhile he's waiting," the Pasionaria explained.

The explanation was followed by a short silence.

"Well, there it is," said Margherita at last. "That's the idea. Would it go as a point of departure?"

I replied that it had gone.

They were, all three of them, much mortified.

The Pasionaria handed me another candy; then, while Margherita and Albertino held a whispered discussion, she told me that things had in fact turned out very differently. "He's one, not two, and he's waiting for the telephone call from her. The other one doesn't come into it."

The story began to interest me.

"Then the other one," I said, "doesn't go out at all?"

"Of course not!" cried the Pasionaria. "If he doesn't come into it, how can he go out? And she's the one who's determined that he go out with her. He isn't. The other one is, because he's waiting for the telephone call."

"Who's she then?"

"The wife of the one who's away. At Cuneo."

"What's he doing at Cuneo?"

"That I couldn't tell you," said the Pasionaria. "I don't even know what Cuneo looks like. He's waiting for the telephone call from his wife, and then his daughter comes home from school."

The story was taking on substance.

"Then the telephone man," I said, "has a daughter?"

"Of course! But he also has a wife because they're the father and the mother of the daughter. Then the daughter comes home from school and her father is still waiting for the telephone call, so they talk. The little girl is unhappy and her father is sorry about it."

"That means he must be a good man," I said.

"Fairly good," the Pasionaria answered. "He's sorry his daughter is unhappy and he asks her what's happened but she begins to cry. Then she has a temperature and she has to go to bed and the doctor comes."

I asked if it was anything serious.

"Serious enough," said the Pasionaria, "because she's a very delicate little girl and having a temperature is a serious illness. But she didn't get it because she was sick, she got it because she was unhappy."

The Pasionaria was quite moved by all this; her eyes filled with tears.

"And the temperature," she went on, "kept getting worse and worse and the little girl was just about to die."

It was a nasty business all right, and had mysterious aspects as well. I couldn't understand, for instance, why a little girl would run the risk of dying because she was unhappy.

"She couldn't help it," the Pasionaria told me. "She was a little girl and little girls can't stand being unhappy. Women can stand it because they're grown up, but not delicate little girls. So, anyway, meanwhile the little girl kept on crying and her father didn't know what was wrong. Then he opened her school box and there was her report card with terrible marks."

"A little girl ought to be unhappy if she gets bad grades," I said. "But there's no reason for her to get sick because she's unhappy."

"That's the kind of little girl she was, and it took months and months for her to get well," the Pasionaria concluded with a sigh. "Now the story's over."

But there were still some unresolved points. Did the telephone call ever come? Did the woman get back from Cuneo?

"She didn't go to Cuneo," said the Pasionaria. "She went to Monza to buy a bath sponge."

I got annoyed. What kind of woman would leave Milan, where there must be two thousand shops that sell bath sponges, to go to Monza to buy one? Why?

The Pasionaria shrugged her shoulders.

"She says they cost less there," she muttered, "because that's where the factory is. She's always doing things like that. Don't you remember when we went to Rome and she wanted to go by way of Turin to buy a silk handkerchief to put on her head because they don't cost as much in Turin as they do in Milan?"

"That's right," I said.

I sat looking at the typewriter keys for a while. Then I asked in a low voice: "What about the report card?"

The Pasionaria spoke into my ear. "I put it in the desk

drawer for you. There's no need for *that* one to see it. You can sign it and tomorrow I'll take it back."

Meanwhile, *that* one had finished her conversation with Albertino and now came over to join us.

"He isn't waiting for a telephone call," Margherita said. "He isn't even home, he's in a café drinking a glass of brandy."

"That brandy's a bad idea," I replied. "He'll get heartburn afterwards, as he always does. What's she doing?"

"She's not in Milan any more," Margherita said. "She's gone to Argentina."

"How sad," I murmured, "to be so far from her native land, in a strange country."

Margherita held out her hands.

"It's fate," she said, and she sounded terribly sad.

THE ENERGETIC EDUCATOR

I knew a savage of a man. He lived on the outskirts of Milan, in a small house, where he had furnished an enormous attic for himself, and there he worked, and sometimes he even slept there, because the children annoyed him, his wife annoyed him, the cat annoyed him.

Everything, in a word, annoyed him. Then too, he would never allow anyone to touch his things, to move a piece of paper, or a pen, or a book.

Like a hawk in its nest, this savage hovered as a constant threat over the whole house. He had a telephone that was connected with the kitchen, on the ground floor, and every once in a while he would lift the receiver and bawl out that he wanted a cup of coffee.

Now this savage had two tender young children: a boy of ten and a little girl under seven, and it was she, above all, who was the victim of his brutality.

This little girl, who was less than seven years old, was small, slight, almost sickly, yet she was forced to climb three steep flights of steps carrying in her right hand a heavy saucer with a cup full of coffee and in her left a huge album of illustrated stories. Ought she to have been bawled out if the coffee, overflowing from the saucer into which, by the force of circumstances, it had become transferred, dripped a little bit on the stairs?

Yet this savage did bawl her out.

The most horrifying scenes usually took place over the paste.

This brutish man was both intolerant and impetuous and, when he looked for his jar of paste and couldn't find it, turned into a madman.

He would not admit that either for pleasure or for profit a child might like to collect those agreeable colored pictures, of a historic, geographic, or philatelic nature, which these days constitute one of the chief prides and joys of children. The pictures are supposed to be pasted into albums made for this purpose, and of course, paste is essential. But this savage despised all such things. All he wanted was his jar of paste. And he wanted it at once; every moment of waiting brought forth a fresh howl.

One day a shriek was heard: "The paste!" And the brutish man descended like an avalanche into the kitchen. The little girl was sitting on the floor, working on her collection of pictures. The man hurled himself like a beast upon the paste jar, but when he had it in his hands, an inhuman cry was torn from his throat: "It's empty!"

The mother, who rose with the dawn, had done all her heavy housework and was now allowing herself a few moments of relaxation with an innocent little murder story. She raised her head.

"It's empty!" shrieked the man. "The jar of paste is empty! And I have two hundred clippings to paste up! And today is Sunday! It's empty!"

The mother attempted to calm the demented man with a word of wisdom. "It would be empty," she observed, "even if today were Monday."

"If today were Monday," shouted the man, "the stationery shops would be open and I could buy another jar!"

Still in the voice of a man possessed he turned on the little girl.

"This time," he howled, "you're going to get a lesson you'll remember the rest of your life!"

Then a terrible thing happened.

The man unbuckled the heavy leather belt he wore and drew it slowly from his trousers: slowly, because he wanted to prolong the sadistic pleasure he derived from the infamous act he was about to perform.

He doubled the belt, so as to render it shorter and

heavier, and dealt a blow of bestial force. The buckle struck the table, shattered a porcelain ashtray, and dented the wood.

The man dealt another blow at the table, breaking the other ashtray and a vase. It was at that moment that the truly irrevocable thing occurred: the man's trousers slipped down.

The mother raised her eyes from her book.

"You'll have to get some new underwear," she remarked. "Those shorts are worn out."

The man drew up his trousers and put his belt back on.

He looked fiercely around the room. In one corner stood the broom. He grabbed it with both hands and broke the handle across his knee. Brandishing the stick, he advanced slowly on the little girl. But suddenly he stopped and turned to the mother.

"Look at her!" he shouted. "That wretched creature is laughing!"

"Naturally," said the mother. "When you pulled your trousers up, you left your shirttail out."

At this the man was seized with a murderous fury. In one villainous stroke of the stick, he smashed the vase on the mantle. The stick flew out of his hands, so he advanced on the gas stove and kicked it.

The little girl, in her corner of the room, went on arranging her pictures.

"That's what I'm going to do to you!" the man shouted at the little girl. "I'll teach you to touch things that belong to me!"

At this he remembered the paste again and banged his fist savagely on the table.

"An empty paste jar! Two hundred clippings to paste up! And the stores closed because today is Sunday!"

The little girl looked up from her pictures for a moment.

"Actually, it's Saturday," she said, "and the stationery store is open."

The mother got up.

"You've done an unworthy thing, Giovannino!" she cried. "You've accused your daughter of its being Sunday."

The man stood confused for a moment, then lost his temper altogether.

"Never mind!" he shouted. "That's the way she learns, even if it *is* Saturday!"

"Children don't learn through brutality," Margherita said coldly.

The man headed sullenly toward the stairs.

"And tuck your shirttail in," said Margherita.

"I want my paste!" said the man.

"You'll get it," Margherita said. "We'll go out and buy it now. Then you can paste up your silly newspaper clippings."

Twenty minutes later the man telephoned down from his lair. The little girl answered.

"My paste!" cried the man. "Has it come yet?"

"Yes, but right now I'm using it for my pictures," she replied, putting down the receiver.

FORBIDDEN FRIES

I was as dilapidated as an old Ford: defective carburetor, stomach cylinder out of order, irregular flow of oil, heart beating in the head, wiring that kept fusing. Now a foot, now a hand, now an elbow or knee, now a headlight burned out, now the nose, now the teeth, now the spine. Nothing was right.

I tried bicarbonate of soda, pills, pomades, gargles, powders, DDT, alcohol, iodine, tablets, purges, tonics, sulfa drugs, mustard plasters, compresses, inhalations, fumes, oil, naphtha, milk, mineral water, fruit salts, infusions, phosphates, and yogurt.

One day I called my family together, and I said: "The situation is serious. The machine keeps going by dint of wire and string, and I can't send it to the garage because I can't take it out of use. So everybody's got to do his bit to help. From today on, the house is going to be reorganized. For six days of the week everybody behaves as his own sense and discretion dictate, but on Monday Papa has to be allowed to run like clockwork. Papa works Sunday night, and he works Monday night, and inasmuch as he also works all day Monday, nothing, all day Monday, must be allowed to interfere with him. Now, to go like clockwork, he needs two things: absolute tranquillity and adequate food. Six days of the week Papa can have a stomach ache, Monday he can't."

Albertino and the Pasionaria accepted this without thinking that it was an attempt to inaugurate a dictatorship on my part. And they agreed to cooperate.

To avoid all misunderstanding, the Pasionaria asked for elucidation of certain details.

"Monday," she said "is it all right for you to get mad if you don't find the paste on your desk? Or if I'm using the drawing paper and the India ink?"

"No," I replied. "I can get mad only on account of the paste, which is something I don't need very often. But since I've got to do some drawings every Monday, the absence of the essential materials, such as paper and ink, will not be tolerated."

"That's all right," agreed the Pasionaria. "That only means I'll have to change days."

Albertino had only one question. "Is it all right for you to get mad on Monday if you don't find any more oranges to make an orangeade with?"

"No," I replied, "it is not. The absence of orangeade could endanger the entire working operation."

"Very well," Albertino said in an easy voice. "Mondays I'll make do with apples or pears."

Margherita appeared to have no objections. But when I thought I had everything arranged, she cried: "So I'm a Lucrezia Borgia, am I? Seven days of the week I poison my husband, and now he asks, as a special favor, that I don't poison him on Mondays."

This was not what I meant.

"It's merely a question," I said clearly, "at Monday's

meals, of avoiding foods that are not suitable to my particular gastric disturbances. For instance, absolutely no fried foods on Mondays."

We were in the kitchen, and my India ink and brushes were, naturally enough, on the kitchen table, where the Pasionaria was making use of them for her own purposes.

"Today's not Monday," the Pasionaria told me when I asked her for the ink and a brush.

"I know that," I replied. "I only want my ink as a temporary loan, so I can write on the wall above the gas stove: 'Mondays in this house, nothing gets fried.' "

After I had posted this announcement, Margherita shook her head in a melancholy manner. "So we're going to start all over again with writing on the wall, are we? Why don't you also write that Italy's destiny lies on the sea and that she'll never turn back?"

With a sad heart I felt constrained to rebuke her for her inopportune sarcasm. "By safeguarding my stomach on Mondays, I'm safeguarding my work, and the future of our children!"

It was the first Monday after the reform.

I had worked all night Sunday, and when I got up from my chair, I found enough oranges to quench my thirst.

I went back upstairs and sat down at my drawing table. All the brushes were in the yellow jar, and beside them stood the bottle of India ink. Instead of the pot of paste, I found a note from the Pasionaria: "The paste is on my desk. Don't worry, go and get it."

I had no need for it, so I didn't worry and I didn't go and get it.

Everything went wonderfully well. At one o'clock the

inside telephone rang, and when I picked up the receiver, Margherita said that if I wanted to come down, luncheon was served. But before I heard Margherita's voice, I smelled the hideous odor of frying food. Some people would doubtless say the smell did not come into the studio along the telephone wire but through the crack under the door, but I am convinced the stench was so strong I smelled it through the telephone.

I went down, and coughing my way through the smoke in the kitchen, sat down at my place. I said nothing, but the Pasionaria, who had just come home from school, threw her satchel on a chair and shouted: "I could smell it as soon as I turned off Viale Romagna. 'Mondays in this house, nothing gets fried!' "

Margherita, who had just finished burning God knows what in the frying pan, turned.

"Monday?" she cried. "I thought today was Saturday. It's extraordinary how much Saturday is like Monday here in Milan!"

I was not going to get excited.

"The days pass, one after the other," I said, "and so much alike, it's easy to lose all idea of time. Anyway, it won't happen again. Every Monday morning I'm going to put up a sign saying, 'Notice: Today is Monday.' "

I ate the fried food and soon had a stomach ache, but I didn't feel too bad, for I was convinced it was my last Monday stomach ache.

It was the following Monday. Early in the morning I went down to the kitchen to squeeze some oranges, and on the rack above the stove I affixed the sign: "Notice: Today is Monday."

I came down again at one, and Margherita was at the stove, frying something.

I got angry.

"Margherita," I asked, "did you happen to see a sign reading, 'Notice: Today is Monday'?"

"Yes," she replied cheerfully. "It was a kind thought. Of course you might also have written, 'Tomorrow is Tuesday.' But I couldn't understand why you wanted to tell me that today is Monday."

"Mondays in this lousy house, nothing gets fried!" cried the Pasionaria, throwing her satchel into a corner of the room.

Then Margherita remembered, and so great was her consternation that I said nothing more. Once again I ate fried food and had a stomach ache and a hard time working that afternoon and night.

It was the third Monday after the reform, and I went downstairs at lunchtime to find that Margherita was not frying anything—because she'd already finished.

In silence I awaited the return of the Pasionaria. She tossed her satchel on the radiator.

"Mondays in this house, nothing gets fried!" cried the Pasionaria in a disgusted tone. "Only on the day after Sunday and the day before Tuesday."

I turned to Margherita.

"Didn't you see the sign," I asked, "telling you what day it is?"

Margherita spread out her arms and raised her eyes to the ceiling.

"Yes," she answered, "yes, I saw the Monday notice, I read the notice that Monday nothing gets fried, but I decided for once I'd allow myself to disobey the order. How's a poor woman to prepare lunch and dinner if she's not allowed to fry anything? A poor woman who's never taken courses in cooking, who racks her brain trying to think of dishes that aren't fried, isn't she allowed once in her life to make some fried food? It's inhuman!"

The fourth Monday after the reform, I sat down at the table at one o'clock in the best of humor. Margherita had cooked up a panful of fried stuff that could be smelled as far away as San Babila, but I was in the best of humor. When the Pasionaria came home and cried, "Mondays in this house, nothing gets fried," I didn't get angry, I felt more cheerful than ever. Margherita brought to the table the customary vat of minestrone, the kind I love, which bloats me so and which I must never eat.

"No, thank you," I said when the soup was passed to me.

"Aren't you eating?" Margherita asked. "Aren't you feeling well?"

"I'll eat. I'm waiting."

I didn't have long to wait. After about five minutes there was a ring at the door and a waiter in a white jacket appeared, carrying a tray in his hands. He took from the tray a plate of baked pasta, a plate of plain meat with vegetables, and a saucer of stewed fruit. With something of a flourish, he arranged it all in front of me, and left. I began to eat quietly, pretending not to see the look on Margherita's face.

"This," she said, vibrating with indignation, "is the most frightful insult a man can pay the mother of his children! He may go out to eat in a restaurant—all right—but having a restaurant bring food into his own house, that, I honestly believe, has never happened before!"

The baked pasta was just as I like it: a small portion, not at all rich, and very tasty. I went on to the rest of the meal, paying not the slightest heed to Margherita. When I finished, I said: "Margherita, on Mondays I have to run like clockwork—not for myself but for the future of my children, and also for yours. If by some evil chance we always have to have fried food on Monday, then that's an obstacle I must overcome—at any cost!"

"Don't try to cover up what you've done," she said bitterly. "I consider it a gross offense."

And that's the way things stood when I went back upstairs to work. It was rather unpleasant, but my stomach was fine.

The fifth Monday I went downstairs prepared for combat. Entering the kitchen, I smelled nothing frying. I smelled nothing, in fact. Somebody had laid the table, but the general impression was that no meal had been cooked. Margherita was listening to the radio. Albertino was outside in the garden. When the Pasionaria arrived, even she was dumbfounded.

"Well!" she cried crossly. "Isn't there ever going to be anything more to eat in this horrible house?"

Margherita paid no attention to her. Obviously the storm was going to break with the arrival of the waiter bringing my lunch.

But nothing broke. The waiter arrived with a large hamper, brought out four plates of baked pasta, four plates of boiled meat with vegetables, and four bowls of stewed fruit. He arranged them on the table and left.

We sat down to eat in silence.

At last, with the fruit, Margherita explained: "What a relief, once a week, not to have to mess around with pots and pans! I needed a holiday. Besides, I think it's a good idea to have a change once a week."

Nothing more was said.

The days passed, and it was the sixth Monday after the reform.

At one o'clock I came downstairs and sat down to wait at the table, which had already been set. The boy from the restaurant arrived and arranged the plates: baked pasta, fried brains . . .

"What's this?" I cried. "Fried stuff?"

"I brought what the lady ordered on the telephone," the boy said.

When we were alone, Margherita turned to me.

"Boiled meat! Boiled meat! Always boiled meat!" she cried. "A person gets tired of it. You need a change once in a while!"

The seventh Monday the boy from the restaurant didn't come, because nobody called him. I went downstairs at one o'clock and the house was impregnated with the smell of frying.

When the Pasionaria arrived, she wrinkled up her nose.

"If this frying doesn't stop," she cried, "it's going to end up with me going to a restaurant on Mondays!"

After lunch I took bicarbonate and went upstairs to finish my drawing. I found neither brushes nor pencils nor India ink. Instead there was a note from the Pasionaria: "If the others are going to do what they want, so will I!"

So I came to the conclusion that if that's the way things had to go, maybe it was just as well that that's the way they went and I cheered up. Today is the thirteenth Monday, and out of the kitchen billow gusts of black smoke bearing such an odor of frying as the human nose has never smelled before.

And I thank God that today I have a cold that makes that infernal stench seem altogether innocuous.

"I DONE IT ALL MYSELF"

When I reached home, it was two o'clock in the morning, and I had to ring the bell for at least a quarter of an hour.

Finally Margherita opened the door.

"Have you come back?" she asked.

"No," I said, between clenched teeth.

"I think you're right," she said. "It's always dangerous to travel at night."

Margherita's logic is always of interest. In this particular instance it was downright extraordinary, and I could see that the only thing for me to do was ignore the remark.

When the door was shut, Margherita fell asleep again, and sleeping climbed the steps, entered our room, and got into bed. I peeked into the room and saw that everything was all right: in the bed with Margherita were Albertino, the Pasionaria, and the cat. The Pasionaria opened one eye, with which she gave me a wicked glance.

"Hmm," she muttered, "*he* got back."

I went to another room to sleep and was just turning out the light when Margherita appeared in the doorway.

"Is there any mail for me?" she asked.

"As a matter of fact," I said calmly, "the one who just got home isn't you, it's me. I'm the one who should be asking if there's any mail."

Margherita shook her head.

"No mail," she said in a distant voice. "Though somebody telephoned the other night from Rome."

"I know," I said. "That was me. I called to see if everybody was all right . . . "

"And what did they tell you?" Margherita asked.

"That everybody was all right."

"Thank God," Margherita murmured. "Now I can rest easier."

She returned to our room, and there was silence.

I was awakened the next morning by a shriek from Margherita. And in she came, waving an exercise book.

"Look at the mark she got on her homework!" she cried. "The teacher wants the parents to sign it, so the brat lets me see it now, two minutes before she's supposed to leave for school. . . . And look at it! She writes 'cuore' with a 'q'!"

The Pasionaria stood in the doorway, waiting for her exercise book.

"She wouldn't let me help her with her homework," Margherita said to me. "She doesn't even want me to look over her homework any more, do you see?"

I saw.

"So she wrote 'cuore' with a 'q' and she got a lower mark than she should have gotten," Margherita went on.

The Pasionaria remained calm.

"The last time she helped me," the Pasionaria said to me, "I got a better mark. This time I got a lower mark, but I done it all myself."

"Did it," I corrected.

" 'Done it' sounds better," the Pasionaria replied with assurance. "You can write 'did' but you say 'done.' "

I insisted: "You never say, 'I done it.' "

"Why didn't you stay in Rome?" asked the Pasionaria.

Margherita shouted that she would never sign the notebook. So I had to sign it, but before I did so, I asked: "Why don't you want your mother to look over your homework?"

"I'll look after my own affairs," answered the Pasionaria. "I'm the one who's going to school, not her."

The principle, though expressed in not quite acceptable terms, was a sound one.

"But if your mother had looked over your homework, you wouldn't have written 'cuore' with a 'q.' She would have corrected it."

"Sure," replied the Pasionaria, "but if I hadn't written it first myself, how could she have corrected it?"

"That's right," I went on, "but if she *had* corrected it,

you wouldn't have gotten such a low mark, you'd have done much better."

The Pasionaria shrugged. "I'd rather have a low mark for work I done myself than a high mark for something somebody else done."

I signed the notebook.

THE ACRE

"Margherita," I said, as I sat down at the table, "do you remember that little farm I was talking about last year?"

"No," Margherita replied. "Why?"

"Because I've bought it."

Margherita looked at me in horror, then turned to the children. "A writer's troubles aren't enough for him, he has to take on a farmer's too."

I told her not to exaggerate. "It's only one acre," I said.

But this, instead of calming her, increased her agitation. "For years now the newspapers have been talking about nothing but acres, and now you have to go and buy one."

It was an example of Margherita's particular brand of argumentation, and by now I should be used to it. But I got annoyed and asked her to stop talking nonsense.

"Nonsense?" she cried. "Occupation of the land, large landowners, agrarian reform, alluvium, and so on and so on—in every political squabble with the farmers, do you or don't you deny that acres are mixed up in it?"

I withdrew from the struggle.

The next morning Margherita asked me: "Well, where is this acre of yours?"

And she wanted to know if it had grass, and did plants grow on it.

A few days later I heard the Pasionaria speaking on the telephone to a little friend.

"No," she said, "I can't tomorrow. Tomorrow we're going to see Papa's acre . . ."

We stopped at the little *trattoria* in the area to eat something. In the next room were men drinking and talking. One of them said: "You know that little piece of ground at the crossroads? Well, it seems the man who bought it has turned up."

"What does he look like?" asked another.

"I haven't seen him. But he must look like a darn fool."

"Sure," added a third. "He paid double what that postage stamp is worth—he must be an idiot."

"No," said an old man, "just a poor ignorant man. He doesn't know anything about it, so they fleeced him."

"If he doesn't know anything about it," said the first man, "he ought to stay home and look after what he does know about. As far as I'm concerned, he's a fool."

"Of course," added a fourth. "He's one of those city squirrels who go for a ride in the country and right away they have to have fresh air and the simple life and all the rest of it. So they buy a piece of land and then they sell it for half what they paid."

They roared with laughter. Then one said: "Funny business! In the city they think of the joys of country living, but when they come out to the country, the first thing they say is they can't live without central heating, they can't live without a bath with hot and cold running water. I'll bet my bottom dollar the people that bought the land at the crossroads will build themselves a villa with a bathroom and central heating and umbrellas in the garden so they can drink their tea in the shade . . . !"

"I won't take the bet. They'll build their villa."

"And she'll be going around in slacks, like at the beach."

They snickered.

"If they build themselves a house, we'll have a laugh!" cried a younger man. "Anybody who'd pay that much money for that piece of land would probably put up a Swiss chalet here, four steps from the Po."

"I know the type. They put up a house, then they start tearing it down. 'Would you mind, I'd like to have that door changed. . . . Board up that window there and make one on the other side. . . . Put up a wall here and tear that one down. . . . ' That's the type that likes to hear people say they're original, even a little crazy. And boy, they know it when the bills start coming in!"

"Well," put in the old man, "why not? If he's got the money, let him spend it as he likes."

"How much can he have? If he were rich, he wouldn't have come around here to build. And he wouldn't have bought one acre. I tell you, he's a nobody."

Margherita shook her head. "What are you going to do now? Sell the acre?"

"No, Margherita. As soon as I have the money, I'm going to build a house with a bath and central heating and a flower garden. And every once in a while I'll change my mind, and I'll say, 'Would you mind moving that door two feet to the right? Close up that window and open one on the opposite wall. . . . ' That's the fate of us nobodies."

Margherita sighed, then said that after all, everything considered, she rather liked the idea.

"It'll be nice to be able to get away from the city," she said, "into this marvelous peace, among these simple, friendly people—these people who understand us so well. . . . "

THE CHILDREN ARE
WATCHING US

I was taking the air at the window that gave out on the garden. Behind the bars of the gate I saw the mailman putting something into the letter box. At that moment the Pasionaria appeared out of nowhere and went humming to the gate. She opened the letter box and took out a newspaper and several letters.

Unaware that I was watching her, she behaved in a

completely natural manner: she tucked the newspaper under her arm, opened the letters, read them, and put them back in the envelopes.

I heard Albertino calling: "Anything there?"

"Nothing," the Pasionaria replied, in a tone of annoyance. "All his stuff."

She came into the house, left the letters and the newspaper, and went back out.

A little later, at the table, I brought the matter up.

"Margherita," I said, "did the mail come?"

"I didn't look in the box," Margherita said.

"I did," announced the Pasionaria. She got the letters and the newspaper. "There was only this junk here."

"How odd!" I cried. "Does the mail arrive in this condition now? I'm going to write a letter of protest to the postmaster. I'll have the mailman fired—he'll learn not to open my letters."

The Pasionaria shook her head. "It wasn't him that opened them," she said. "It was me."

I looked at the envelopes, one by one, then showed them to the Pasionaria.

"But they're all addressed to me," I said. "Why did you open them?"

Without the slightest hesitation, the Pasionaria replied: "I had to. She wasn't here when they arrived, so I opened them."

"Inconceivable!" I cried. "Are you suggesting that your mother opens letters addressed to me?"

"Of course," replied the Pasionaria.

"Of course nothing!" I cried. "This is something new!"

The Pasionaria gave me a compassionate smile.

"Something new!" she repeated. "Just imagine! Then

why are you always hollering at her for opening your letters?"

I had her right where I wanted her.

"Exactly!" I hollered. "And if I holler at your mother because I don't want her to open my letters, why do *you* open them?"

"Oh, you're always hollering," she replied, shrugging her shoulders. "That's all you ever do."

This was too much.

"Do you dare to criticize your parents?" I said.

"Not criticize," said the Pasionaria. "Listen."

Here Margherita intervened. "The children are watching us," she declared in a tone of bitter irony. "Don't forget it, Giovannino."

"No, Margherita," I said, "I won't forget it. And when they see their mother shamelessly continuing to open letters addressed to her husband even though he's asked her not to, it's only natural for them to open letters addressed to their father or to their mother."

"No," the Pasionaria corrected me, "they don't open letters addressed to their mother."

"Why not?"

"Because you don't open letters addressed to Mama. If her own husband doesn't open them, why should her children?"

It was logic all right, and I felt the full impact of its ghastly lack of logic.

"Very well," I said. "Then why open my letters? If you're your mother's children, aren't you also your father's children?"

Albertino was struck by my clear and cogent argument

and indicated that he approved it unconditionally. The Pasionaria, however, had something more to say.

"I don't open my father's letters, I open the letters that come for my mother's husband. Father and mother are the same, they're the parents. But the husband doesn't concern the children, he concerns the wife."

I refused to countenance this.

"For children," I said, "parents are exclusively father and mother. And children must see their parents exclusively as father and mother."

The Pasionaria was not so easily vanquished.

"My mama," she said, "is always my mama even though she's your wife. But my papa, like when he upsets my mama, isn't my papa any more but my mama's husband."

"And how about when your mother upsets me?" I cried indignantly. "Who gets upset, her husband or your father?"

"Her husband," was the Pasionaria's cynical reply. "That's *her* affair, I don't want to get mixed up in it."

The conclusion was both terrible and inescapable.

"Then all this means," I said, "that while your mother, for you, is always your mother, I am sometimes your father and sometimes a man who has no direct connection with you but with your mother. Sometimes, in other words, I'm a stranger to you!"

The Pasionaria evidently found my reasoning somewhat difficult to follow, for she remained silent for a time, thinking it over. Then she came to a decision.

"When I was born, you weren't there," she said. "You came back later. But Mama was there."

"So what?" cried Albertino. "It's the men who go to war, not the women!"

"What's that got to do with it?" said the Pasionaria with a shrug. "If women went to war, then my papa would have been home and my mama would have been in the war and I wouldn't have been born."

The Pasionaria left with her brother, and when she said "So long" to me, I didn't know whether she was speaking to her father or the husband of her mother.

When I got home at noon the next day, I found seven letters beside my plate, all properly sealed. I derived considerable satisfaction from this—and the Pasionaria appeared to derive considerable surprise. I was aware of her glances as I opened the envelopes with a knife. I was content.

But the next day, unfortunately, I got home a little before noon, and as I crossed the hall I saw Margherita standing over the gas stove in the kitchen, holding an envelope over a kettle of boiling water.

The Pasionaria was watching her.

I went out and stayed out a good half hour.

When I sat down at the table, I found three letters beside my plate. They were all sealed.

After lunch, the children left, and I said to Margherita: "I saw you opening my letters like a concierge. With the little girl right there. Fine tricks you teach your daughter!"

Margherita looked around.

"I didn't teach it to her," she said. "She showed me how to open the envelopes that way."

"Margherita, this is terrible."

"She's the one," Margherita whispered. "She's been

after me all morning. She said I let my husband walk all over me, she said I'm spineless!"

"Margherita, you're treading on dangerous ground. You must not listen to her."

"I don't know what to do," Margherita murmured. "I don't know what to do. Giovannino, try to understand!"

I tried to understand.

ADMINISTRATION

On my first night home after being away on business for a week, I was relaxing after supper when the Pasionaria turned off the radio. I told her to turn it on again because there was something I wanted to hear.

"Later," she said. "First we have to have the meeting."

"Meeting?" I was bewildered. "Is this something new?"

"No, it's nothing new," replied Margherita, coming up with two ledgers and some pens. "Now we have a meeting every night after supper. We began it right after you left."

Margherita sat down and opened a ledger.

"The evening meeting," she said, "is divided in two parts: balancing the books for the past twenty-four hours and estimating the budget for the next twenty-four hours."

I confessed that although everything was as clear as it could be I didn't understand a word of it. Margherita then took it upon herself to enlighten me.

"Until now," she said, "we've been living like a family of horses pasturing in the meadow and eating what we find without a thought for the morrow. We've never had an administration. A house without an administration is like a building without a foundation—it stays up because it stays up, but nobody guarantees its stability. But now our house has an administration. This is very important, above all because the children take part in the evening discussion and thus get a precise idea of how much it costs to run a family and they learn to distinguish between what is essential and what is unnecessary. They don't grow up packed in cotton wool, they become aware of the various difficulties that must be overcome in order to live."

I felt enormous admiration for Margherita.

"The children," she went on, "understand the basic concept to perfection. You," she said, "you tell Papa what a house is, speaking administratively."

The Pasionaria recited, all in one breath: "A house, administratively speaking, is a ship whose crew consists of a father who does the rowing, a mother who holds the tiller, and children who don't lie around sleeping but help their father and their mother and thus learn to row and to navigate. Amen."

"This is no time for joking," Margherita reproved her. "The meeting is now open. Are there any suggestions or observations on the management of the past twenty-four hours? Was the money that was spent, well spent?"

The Pasionaria and Albertino looked at each other.

"As far as I'm concerned," said Albertino, "yes."

"As far as I'm concerned," said the Pasionaria, "the money that was spent on minestrone was wasted. I like spaghetti better."

Margherita tossed her head.

"So when I boil a chicken," she said, "am I supposed to throw the broth away? Come on, are there any other observations? Could any savings have been effected?"

"Too much salt in the soup," muttered the Pasionaria.

Margherita refused to accept the provocation.

"We will now," she said, "pass on to the estimate for tomorrow. Take notice that your father is now present. You, write!"

Albertino, with a grinding of his teeth, grasped a pen and at the head of a fresh page wrote: "Thursday, March 5. Potential forces, four. Actual forces, four." Then he read it aloud.

"Very well," said Margherita in a crisp, almost military voice. "Now, Albertino, list the various requirements."

Albertino listed:

"Four requirements of bread at breakfast, four at lunch, two for afternoon tea, and four at dinner. Total, fourteen."

"Thirteen," corrected the Pasionaria. "I want a requirement of polenta at dinner."

"Impossible," declared Margherita, "because uneconomic. Either all bread or all polenta."

Four requirements of polenta were then approved for the evening meal.

"Every requirement," Margherita explained to me, "whether for bread or anything else, is expressed in both quantity and cost. We've made a complete reference book."

Both the type of soup and its accompaniment having

been agreed upon, the administrative council then determined the relative requirements.

"We also," observed the Pasionaria, "need a requirement for the cat."

"The cat is not included among the forces," Margherita declared. "The cat will have to make do with what's left over. We will now list the totals. How much are we going to spend for tomorrow's food?"

Albertino and the Pasionaria worked for quite a while over the addition and came up at the end with a result that did not please Margherita.

They did the problem over and achieved a second result remarkably different from the first, but Margherita liked it no better. She shook her head.

"Two hundred lire more than today," she said. "That won't do. Tomorrow we'll have to make our choice with greater care. Meanwhile, inasmuch as we have to make up the deficit, we will remove the two hundred lire from the fixed quota estimated for Group B."

Margherita took this opportunity to explain Group B to me.

"We've established how much we ought to spend annually for clothes, linen, shoes, laundry, cleaning, assorted repairs, light, heating, gas, domestic service, recreation, travel, studies, cigarettes, culture, taxes, weekends, amortization of capital, tips, stamps, drugs, upkeep of the house, and so on. Then we added it all up and divided by three hundred and sixty-five, in order to establish how much we ought to spend daily. That's Group B. There's another ledger for Group B, listed according to item."

As I turned over the pages of the Group B ledger, I felt a growing horror.

"Margherita," I said, "did you establish this administration?"

"No, Signora Marcella established it, using as a basis her own family, which is the same size as ours. Naturally, it's been adapted to our particular way of life. It's a masterpiece of precision. You can be absolutely sure that when conditions are normal, as they are now, the house and the family will come to this figure daily."

I looked at the figure, which was colossal, outrageous.

"Margherita," I stammered, "I couldn't possibly spend an amount like this every day."

Margherita smiled.

"Really, Giovannino," she said, "you're arguing like a man who has a car and says, 'My car does ten kilometers on a liter of gas, and since gas costs a hundred and thirty lire a liter, I'm spending thirteen lire a kilometer.' But what about the oil? the tires? repairs? taxes? insurance? amortization of capital? Think about it for a minute, Giovannino."

I thought about it: Margherita was right.

I was dismayed.

"Margherita," I moaned, "it's frightening."

The Pasionaria broke in. "A requirement of cognac for the gentleman!"

Cognac was brought and I drank it down.

"You may have another, Giovannino," Margherita told me. "It's in the budget under the sum appropriated for liabilities."

The cognac picked me up, and I was able to study the Group B ledger somewhat more calmly. Every sum appeared to be hideously precise.

I realized that every day of my life was costing me an

unimaginable amount of money. I had never thought about it before, and now I felt I was carrying a tremendous weight on my shoulders.

"Margherita," I said finally. "Administratively speaking, the family is a boat where the father rows, the mother holds the tiller, and the children help and so learn to row and navigate. All this is absolutely correct. But if the poor oarsman must, in addition to rowing the boat, also every time he dips his oar take into consideration the agitation his oar causes in the liquid mass, and the number of calories consumed by his efforts, and equate them with the volume of air breathed, the number of red corpuscles, the variations of nervous tension, the vitamins, proteins, toxins, decalcification of the tibia, tension of the sciatic nerve, blood pressure, absorption of ultraviolet rays, pyloric reactions, and so on—if he has to do all this, Margherita, can you guess what this unhappy oarsman is going to do one day?"

"Throw himself in the water," declared the Pasionaria.

"Exactly. Throw himself in the water and die of drowning, but not without first having accurately calculated the volume of liquid displaced."

Margherita spread her hands.

"Don't be like the ostrich, Giovannino," she said, "who hides his head in the sand. You must live *consciously*. And to live *consciously*, there is nothing better than a competent family administration."

I did not agree.

"Margherita," I said, "there is only one family administration that I'll put up with. It's based on the following principle: the father rows lightheartedly, taking pleasure in steering his boat across the vast sea, and the children watch the father rowing and so learn by his example that to cross the sea you have to keep rowing."

"What about the mother?" Albertino asked. "What does she do?"

Margherita poured out a requirement of cognac and hurled the Group A and Group B ledgers into the fire.

She rose.

"The mother," she said, "removes the inconvenience of her presence. She abandons the tiller and departs."

"Potential force: four," murmured the Pasionaria. "Actual force: three. Force that will stay in bed until eleven in the morning: one."

Margherita disappeared, and the little boat, now pilotless, foundered along with all its crew on an enormous fruitcake that was brought to the table under the heading of *liabilities*.

CICCIOLATA

One evening, cicciolata popped into my mind. Now, cicciolata, which is a little bit like a very hard head cheese, is a delicious dish if you like it. I like it, or at least I used to.

"What do you know?" I said. "I've got a terrible yen to eat cicciolata with polenta."

"Tomorrow," Margherita replied, "I'll have cicciolata and polenta."

But on the morrow I had neither cicciolata nor polenta, and I asked Margherita to bear in mind that I wanted to eat cicciolata and polenta. The following day, at both lunch and dinner, cicciolata and polenta were spoken of again because at neither lunch nor dinner were cicciolata and polenta served. The day after that, history repeated itself, and Margherita lost all patience.

"Cicciolata with polenta, polenta with cicciolata!" she cried, exasperated. "Always cicciolata and polenta! Always polenta and cicciolata! No one can eat cicciolata and polenta his whole life long, there has to be a change once in a while!"

As usual, the initiative, with its corresponding advantage, had passed to Margherita. And Margherita exhibited herself, before the tribunal of public opinion, as a martyr of cicciolata and polenta. I realized how inadequate I was to maintain a discussion with so underhanded an adversary, and resolved, therefore, to act. The next day I went to see my friend Antonio.

"I want to have a pig butchered," I told him.

"I'll take care of it," he said. "I've got just the pig for you, and I know a man who'll prepare it. Which parts do you want for yourself?"

I told him to have the sausages made as he thought best.

"The only thing that really interests me," I said, "is the cicciolata, which has now become a matter of principle. For a whole month I've been asking my wife for a quarter of a pound of cicciolata, and I can't get it. So I'm going to bring pounds of it home. I don't care about anything but the cicciolata—its significance is no longer gastronomic, it's become a moral question!"

So we agreed that Antonio would have the pig slaughtered and prepared, keeping it all at his house to season, and would send me, when it was ready, the slab of cicciolata.

I went home content and spoke no more of cicciolata. In all serenity I waited the five or six days, and when Antonio called me to say that he had found the book I wanted, I raced over in my car.

Antonio showed me the sausages hanging from the ceiling of his kitchen, and tried to explain to me, in full detail, from what point of view he had chosen the sausages best suited to my temperament and to the character, both quantitative and qualitative, of my family. He wanted also to tell me all about the rest of the stuff, still under salt and waiting to be worked, but I interrupted him.

"The cicciolata!" I cried.

He took me, then, down to the cellar and presented the cicciolata to me.

No one, I'm sure, has any idea how much cicciolata you can get out of a six-hundred-pound pig. Before I saw that slab of cicciolata, I had no very precise idea either, to tell the truth, and I may say I was agreeably surprised. I will not be seduced into attempting a description: to get a picture of the thing, one need only think of a slab of granite about six by sixteen by twenty inches. The comparison, however, is not quite precise. A slab of granite is only a slab of granite, while a slab of cicciolata is made of cicciolata, which is infinitely more durable than granite, and somewhat harder to digest.

I stowed the slab away in the luggage compartment of the car and headed home. I parked the car under the portico, near the kitchen door, and with seeming indifference awaited the dinner hour. Fate was on my side. That evening, instead of the usual pasta, there appeared on the table a smoking plate of polenta, as big and round and golden as an August moon.

"At last!" I cried joyously. "Tonight we eat polenta with fresh cicciolata!"

Margherita's expression might almost have been called fierce.

"Are we starting that all over again?" she said. "If you want cicciolata, you have to tell me ahead of time."

"Cicciolata with polenta tonight!" I cried again.

I had arranged things, naturally, with the precision of a chronometer, and no sooner had I pronounced the word "polenta" than the kitchen door opened and Albertino and the Pasionaria entered, bearing a huge carving board on which reposed the granite-like slab of cicciolata. I put the slab right in the center of the table. There was something majestic, even monumental, about it, and Margherita looked at it with amazement and respect—almost, indeed, with awe.

We all ate cicciolata and polenta until we couldn't eat any more. Margherita made no comment: I had outmaneuvered her.

At lunch the next day, naturally enough, we ate cicciolata with polenta. At dinner, polenta with cicciolata. I said nothing. Nor did I say anything the following day, when both at lunch and at dinner the menu consisted exclusively of cicciolata with polenta.

I held out valiantly for three more days. Then, seeing the slab of cicciolata reappear on the table, I was unable to resist saying: "Really—"

"Well!" cried Margherita, paralyzing me with a glance. "When there's no cicciolata, he makes a scene because there's no cicciolata, and when there's cicciolata, he makes a scene because there *is* cicciolata. Would you be kind enough to specify what you expect of us?"

I said I had made no scene and I had no intention of making a scene. The word "really," which I had just uttered, was the beginning of a sentence that had nothing to do with cicciolata.

Margherita calmed down, and I ate the cicciolata.

The next day, when at both lunch and dinner she saw me eat the cicciolata and polenta without saying a word, she grew positively cheerful.

"Giovannino," she said, "you can't imagine how satisfying it is that at last I've found something you like to eat!"

That night I had a long discussion with myself. I considered what still remained of the slab of cicciolata— from the point of view not of its material consistency but of the absorptive abilities of Margherita, Albertino, the Pasionaria, and the cat; and I reached the following conclusion: "If I go to Milan tomorrow and stay there for a couple of weeks, when I come back the slab of cicciolata will be gone."

The next day I went to Milan, where I loitered for two full weeks, and came home full of self-confidence and hope for the future. I strolled through the house, checked the water taps and the locks, and at last went into the pantry to look over our food supplies. The slab of cicciolata was there, exactly as I had left it two weeks earlier.

I shuddered with horror.

The Pasionaria came into the pantry to get a slice of cheese. With studied indifference, I asked: "Didn't you eat any of the cicciolata while I was away?"

"No," said the Pasionaria, "we wanted to, but Mama said you like it so well we have to save it for you. So we didn't touch it. When a father likes something, the children must eat something else so he can have what he likes."

I had to commend her spirit of self-sacrifice.

"Anyway," I said, "it's just as well you didn't eat it. That kind of stuff doesn't keep—it must be spoiled by now."

"No," replied the Pasionaria, "Mama called Signor Antonio, and he said in cold weather like this, cicciolata can last a month."

"That's good," I said, though my heart was broken. "You might as well have a good piece of cicciolata now instead of that cheese."

The Pasionaria shook her head.

"No, no," she said. "That stuff is yours. Well, maybe tonight, at supper, we'll eat a bit of it."

So tonight, at supper, I was to eat cicciolata with polenta!

No! It couldn't be—God wouldn't permit it.

I wandered around the house a little. Then, when no one was looking, I grabbed the cat and threw him into the pantry, and locked the door and put the key in my pocket. An hour later I came back to see what had happened. The cat hadn't even touched the cicciolata. I decided to call in the assistance of more intelligent cats. I opened the pantry window and put some pieces of meat on the sill.

As I closed the door behind me, I felt quite hopeful. My house is known far and wide (and rightly so) as a meeting place for all the cats in the neighborhood, cats so hungry and so fearless and of such an enterprising nature that nothing dismays them. Once, when the pantry window was left ajar, a cat tried to claw open a can of condensed milk, and almost succeeded.

I glanced into the courtyard and saw that the cats were arriving as if they had heard, over the radio, the mobilization order. I went upstairs, but soon heard a hideous clamor, and when I got back down I found Margherita looking desperately for the key to the pantry door.

"I must have put it in my pocket without thinking," I said, handing it to her.

She went inside, then almost at once called to me.

"Look!" she said, pointing to the floor.

I had never seen a cat in such a state. I almost failed to recognize, in that quivering bundle of rags, our very own animal.

"Look, Giovannino!" Margherita cried. "Someone left the pantry window open and a swarm of cats came in, intent on pillage and plunder. But Giangi was here, he foresaw the danger. They were ten to one, but who can intimidate a cat like that, with such a sense of duty? He fought like a lion, he didn't give an inch, the claws of the assassins tore him to bits, but he didn't weaken. And now look at him, bleeding and torn, exhausted but victorious. The cicciolata that his master loves has been saved! Saved and untouched! Saved and uncontaminated—the thieves didn't even manage to lay a claw on it. Look at him,

Giovannino, look at the hero who willingly risked his life to defend his master's cicciolata!"

I leaned over to pet the torn little head of the heroic cat, and softly I whispered: "Scoundrel!"

I write this without fear. Let the SPCA come! I say again what I said before: "That cat isn't a hero, he's a scoundrel."

I ate cicciolata that evening, and the next day, and the day after. And I am still eating it. And I can say nothing—or Margherita will accuse me of base ingratitude in the face of so many sacrifices made by a wife and children and cat.

I am the one who's the hero!

I am a thousand times more a hero than the cat. And I have won a far greater victory than the cat, for the slab of cicciolata has been shattered and crumbled and tonight, at dinner, I shall demolish it completely.

I am confident of it, for I have overcome every obstacle in my path—and only God can stop me: not men, or man-made objects, ever!

FAREWELL, SACRED MEMOIRS!

Margherita, who did not come down to dinner, appeared only when I was having my coffee. She seemed overwrought. In her hands was a large notebook.

"The Central Intelligence Agency," she cried sarcastically, "must already have informed you of what's going on. From A to Z!"

"I was only told," I replied, "that you were not to be disturbed because you were writing. That doesn't sound like much in the way of espionage."

"And were you also told," Margherita went on, "that I was writing my memoirs?"

"No."

"Then I'll tell you now!"

I contented myself with a shrug of the shoulders.

"Be honest!" Margherita exclaimed. "You're furious!"

"No, I'm not," I said honestly.

"But you are!" Margherita's tone was belligerent. "You're furious to think I might have a life of my own. You're the only one who's supposed to have a life here—I'm only something fate happened to throw in your path!"

Margherita sighed deeply, then, turning to Albertino, cried imperiously: "A rock!"

Albertino went out and was soon back with a large

rock, which he handed to Margherita. She put the rock on the table.

"A rock!" Margherita cried. "What's a rock? Something that has weight and volume and surface, but no meaning, because it has never had youth, it has no maturity, it will never have an old age. It's something without past, present, or future. Something that's nothing! Put it on a scale and you'll see what its weight is, but the truth is, it has no weight, because it's inert. Ten thousand years of life may sweep over this stone, and all the events of those ten thousand years won't change its weight by a millionth of an ounce. And that, children, that's what I am where your father is concerned. A particle of nothing!"

The Pasionaria had a comment to make. "But if that particle of nothing falls on a man's head, he'll find out just how much of a nothing it is!"

After having destroyed the Pasionaria with a glance, Margherita continued: "And now, Giovannino, listen to me! At a certain point it turns out that that rock isn't a *thing* but a human being. And do you know why? Because it sits down at the desk and writes its own story. A story which, among other things, is highly interesting. Now, is that a rather inconvenient state of affairs for you, or isn't it, Giovannino?"

"No, Margherita, it's not, because I've never thought of you as a rock. I'll read your memoirs, I assure you, with the greatest interest. Your story must at some point become my story—the point where your story and my story become our story."

Margherita shook her head.

"That particular period," she said, "doesn't interest me because it doesn't belong exclusively to me. I intend to omit it in my narrative. What I'm describing, most of all, is my inner life—I analyze my psychological evolution, and external events are recorded only insofar as they have a bearing on that."

"It sounds more and more fascinating, Margherita. I'd like to read it."

Margherita shrugged her shoulders.

"In that case," she said, "I don't mind reading you a few chapters."

She opened the notebook, threw her cigarette into the fire, and began to read aloud.

"I have been told that I was born on a day in August, but I have never been told what color the sky was, or if it had or didn't have color that day. This makes me very unhappy because I'd like to be able to begin these memoirs of mine by saying that when I was born the color of the sky was different from what it usually is. . . ."

Margherita paused.

"You get the idea, Giovannino?"

"I get it," I replied. "It's like that secret, terrifying thought we all have in our hearts: 'I was born on any old day and any old day I'll die.' We are hurt to the quick by the indifference of the universe to the important events of our lives."

"Exactly!" said Margherita, in a tone of satisfaction.

Then the Pasionaria jumped in. "If they didn't tell you the color of the sky, they could at least have told you what year you were born."

"What's the year got to do with it!" said Margherita, annoyed. "I'm trying to write the story of my life, not a report for the Bureau of Vital Statistics."

"If you're going to write the story of your life," declared

the Pasionaria, "you have to begin by saying you were born on such a day in such a month and in such a year. Everybody begins with that."

Margherita's voice grew sharper. "Dates count for nothing! What counts is deeds, ideas—that's what counts!"

But the Pasionaria remained convinced that she was right.

"Dates do too count," she said. "If somebody doesn't know when he was born, how does he know whether he's young or old?"

Albertino broke in. "Mama knows perfectly well when she was born!"

"Then why doesn't she say so?" demanded the Pasionaria. "That way at least people who read the book will know whether the writer was a girl, or a woman, or an old lady, and so they can tell what it's about."

Margherita nodded.

"That's true," she said. "I'll have to change it."

She began again, aloud: "I have been told that I was born on a day in August, nineteen hundred and . . ."

She closed the book and chucked it into the fire.

"It's a very beautiful book," I remarked, "but the end is rather sad."

The Pasionaria went to the fireplace and with the tongs tried to rescue the notebook from the flames that had already begun to devour it. But Margherita pulled the Pasionaria away.

"Have a little respect," she said, in a sad and solemn voice, "for the ashes at least."

THE ANCESTOR

I got back to my cottage in the country, after being away some ten days on business, to find the whole company at the table at three in the afternoon.

"We're having supper," Margherita explained. "We took advantage of your absence to make a few little changes in the meal hours."

I made no comment. My mind was wholly absorbed by the fascinating question: "If they have supper at three in the afternoon, what time do they have lunch, and what time do they have breakfast? And what about five o'clock tea?"

I went upstairs to my study to sort out the briefcase full of useless paper I'd brought back from Milan. I also had to do some accounts, look over bills, and sign checks—things for which I have always had a marked distaste.

I found my salary scattered among the papers. I started to put the notes to one side, to straighten out the ones that were crumpled and pile them one on top of the other. Then I felt a pair of eyes boring straight through me, and I turned.

Margherita was standing in the doorway, looking at me strangely.

"Giovannino," she asked, with a slight edge of pain in her voice, "what is that money?"

I was astonished. Since I'd known her, Margherita had never been the slightest bit interested in money. It made her uneasy; she handled bank notes with the same troubled distaste with which one day, after she found my pistol in a drawer, she held it out to me, dangling from a finger, and said: "Giovannino, get rid of this awful thing!"

I was still more astonished when Margherita took the money from my hands and counted it. Then she rummaged among the papers in the briefcase, found a few more crumpled notes, and asked me once again what that money was.

"My salary," I told her.

"Why do you hide to count it?"

I told her it had never been my habit to count my money standing on the sidewalk or in the middle of the road.

"Why is it all crumpled up and mixed in with your other papers, as though you'd stuffed it in your briefcase in a great hurry? It has never been my impression that companies pay salaries in handfuls of crumpled bills."

I told her that they had, as a matter of fact, given me my salary in a stout envelope, all neatly arranged, but when I needed some money I took the bills from the envelope and then put them back in the briefcase without taking the trouble to stuff them into the envelope first.

"And just where *is* this envelope?"

I tried to remember what on earth I'd done with it. Then finally it came to me.

"I know!" I said. "I used it to put some water in the electric heater in my studio in Milan."

"And do electric heaters," Margherita asked, "now run on water?"

"No, they don't. But I keep a little pan of water on my

electric heater so the air won't get too dry. All the water had evaporated, so I used the envelope as a glass. I remember the whole thing now, because the envelope fell apart on the third trip and the water spilled on the floor."

Margherita accepted this with a shake of the head.

"I see," she said. "But why did you have the pan soldered to the stove?"

"It isn't soldered, it only stands on top."

"Then why, instead of filling the pan by bringing envelopes full of water from the bathroom, didn't you take the pan into the bathroom and fill it by holding it under the faucet?"

I looked at Margherita in astonishment.

"You're absolutely right, Margherita," I said. "Why didn't I? Particularly since the pan has a handle. And if the handle was hot, I could have used the envelope to wrap around it."

Margherita started.

"In other words," she said, "you'd do anything to be freed of that envelope!"

She put a piece of paper over the pile of bank notes.

"Giovannino," she said, "how much was your salary?"

"I don't remember. There were taxes, deductions, advances. Anyway, the money I got is there—you can count it."

Margherita looked at me.

"It's all there?"

"Absolutely."

"But a minute ago you said you took some out of the envelope when you needed it."

After trying futilely to disentangle a far too intricate affair, I cut the whole thing short.

"Margherita," I said, "if you want to check up on me,

all you have to do is ask the management. What I'd like to know is when this madness came over you."

Margherita shook her head.

"No madness has come over me, Giovannino," she said. "I only want you to remember that once we lived happily on a tenth of what you're earning today, and I wouldn't mind in the slightest going back to live in three little rooms and doing without a car and all the other knick-knacks. The only thing that matters is that you shouldn't do anything wrong."

I was eating when Margherita's voice startled me.

"I called Andrea's bank," she said. "Andrea has been in England for two months. So how could he have given you that car?"

I began to laugh, for it was a different Andrea who had given me the car.

"You've got the wrong Andrea, Margherita," I said. And I told her which Andrea it was.

"What's the point, Giovannino," she said, "of mixing things up still worse and bringing in a new Andrea every ten minutes? If you didn't buy the car, where did you get it?"

This time, by heaven, I did lose my temper. I banged my fist on the table.

"Margherita," I cried, "I hope you don't think I'm dishonest!"

Margherita didn't bat an eyelid.

"Now," she said in a cold hard voice, "I know every-thing."

It is not easy for Margherita to speak in a cold hard voice, she speaks in a cold hard voice only in very exceptional circumstances. I was now seriously annoyed.

"Margherita," I said pointedly, "if you know everything, I'd like to know it too."

Margherita turned toward Albertino and looked at him. Albertino nodded. Margherita rose, rummaged through a drawer, sat down again, and handed me an envelope. In the envelope were three pages, yellowed by time, printed at Parma by the "Imperial Printing Office" on April 3, 1805.

"What's all this?" I asked Margherita.

"Read it," Margherita replied.

It was a long, rambling document signed by the chief justice of one of the provincial criminal courts of the time. Three men had been convicted of robbing a gentleman from Parma of a considerable amount of money. Two of the men were condemned to the gallows, and the third, identified as "Giovanni Guareschi of la Fossa," was assigned to "forced labor at the Wheel of Salso in perpetuity."

I looked at Margherita. "Well, what of it?" I asked.

"Giovanni Guareschi of la Fossa," said Margherita. "La Fossa is right in the heart of the region your family came from. This Giovanni Guareschi is unquestionably one of your ancestors."

"That may be, Margherita. And it saddens me to think he ended up grinding salt at Salsomaggiore."

"I hope he escaped," declared the Pasionaria.

Margherita gave her a withering glance.

"Quiet, you!" she cried. "Even if it was your own father who was condemned, justice must run its course."

Here I had to interrupt.

"Margherita," I said, "it wasn't me who was condemned, it was a man of the same name who lived more than a century and a half ago."

"It was your ancestor, Giovannino. The fruit of the tree depends on the nature of the plant and on the kind of food that feeds its roots. And one of your roots, Giovannino, is fed by the poisoned blood of a savage robber!"

"But first," declared the Pasionaria, "you have to know whether he was guilty or not. In my opinion he was condemned by mistake."

Margherita looked at her with contempt.

"Honor," she said, "among thieves!"

I tried to put an end to the discussion, but Margherita was inflexible.

"Giovannino," she said, "I would never have expected anything like this of you. But now I understand so much —your sudden violent starts of surprise, those cold savage gleams I see sometimes in your eyes. . . . Yes, and your taste for salty foods too . . . Nothing ever has enough salt for you! Naturally. There was plenty of salt at Salsomaggiore. Between you and me now there lurks the shadow of that Giovanni who plunged his dagger into an innocent man!"

The Pasionaria broke in: "There's no dagger mentioned!"

"Morally," said Margherita, "it's there."

I tried to effect a compromise, but Margherita was adamant. She wouldn't even allow an appeal.

Albertino was in favor of a new trial to get at the truth. The Pasionaria did not enter the discussion again, though she tried to conclude it.

"I don't care anything about trials," she said. "What I like are people who know what they want. And, anyway, that was the Middle Ages, and the rich were mean to the poor."

Margherita's smile was ironic.

"The children take after their father," she said. "And they have their father's cunning: when they don't know what to say, they bring in social justice and shrug everything off on politics. Blood will tell!"

We sat down to lunch the following day. I had been thinking things over during the night, and I knew how criminals feel. We were silent until the second course arrived. Then Margherita looked at me.

"Take heart!" she cried in a voice warm with emotion. "Take heart, Giovannino! I'm at your side, and together we'll walk the bright path of redemption! The sun has risen again!"

It was raining, but I felt the heat of that bright sun warming the blood in my veins. The pasta had no salt at all, but I had the strength to say it was "perhaps a little too salty."

"You see?" cried Margherita happily. "Now your blood is cleansed of that atavistic poison!"

THE BEST GIFT OF ALL

The doorbell kept ringing. There was always a delivery boy standing there with a telegram, or a bouquet of flowers, or a package. And each time the Pasionaria, for obvious reasons unable to rush out and open the gate, thereby losing her dignity altogether, was forced to wait until Albertino came back with the latest offering.

The Pasionaria has a clearly defined personality, with which she is able to master her years, which now total eight. Her bones are tiny; one need only look at her to know that when she first opened her eyes she tipped the scales at only a little over three pounds. The towering priest who baptized her, seeing the minute creature in front of him, turned to Margherita and said sternly: "You didn't trouble yourself unduly, madam."

Her bones are tiny and she is small of stature, but she has a strong character, and gives evidence of it on every occasion. "She's someone who holds her cards close"— that's what we say of a woman with complete self-control. It is not hard to imagine how much self-control was needed on such an extraordinary occasion as her First Communion.

When she appeared, adorned from head to foot in a white veil, I was awed. There isn't a man in the world who is worse about clothes than I am. This isn't just an attitude, it's a part of my personality—I manage to look badly dressed even when I'm naked. And I particularly admire anyone who wears clothes well, anyone who wears good clothes without either being overwhelmed by them or overwhelming them with the force of his own personality, who never transforms the clothes, as I do, into a mere cortex.

The Pasionaria wore her beautiful white dress with great dignity, and her every gesture was commensurate with the austerity of the white veil. And so, every time the bell rang at the gate, she was content to wait for Albertino.

Telegrams, flowers, packages—and in every package, a present, all pretty things, and thoughtful. Some were downright valuable, some so captivating, like a great rag doll, that even Margherita was unhinged. However, although each gift must have filled her heart with joy, the Pasionaria showed no outward trace of emotion.

(When some day the Pasionaria finds herself kneeling in front of the altar, and the priest asks her if she will take this man as her lawful wedded husband, the Pasionaria will reply with kindly indifference, "Oh, yes. . . . ")

Margherita was indignant.

"All these people," she cried, "have sent you splendid presents to make you happy, and you don't even take the trouble to smile."

The Pasionaria was not discomposed.

"When people buy a present," she said, "they buy a present *they* like. Let *them* smile."

Fundamentally, the Pasionaria is always right—most especially when she's wrong. Someone who buys a present buys a thing he likes, so he's really giving the present to himself—for what pleases us most in life is not to possess and use a thing we like but to have the power to buy it. Conquest is what counts. And then to give the thing we've bought is still another pleasure, and a greater one than to receive it, for suffering even agreeable things is always somewhat humiliating. In the case of gifts, the things suffered are not always agreeable.

The Pasionaria suffered all her gifts—she suffered them majestically, without being even a particle affected by them. When at last the flood of gifts had abated, there arrived an enormous paper-wrapped package within a wooden crate. To open it, both pliers and hammer were required.

And out of the chips of wood and the corrugated paper rose a glittering blue bicycle.

We all turned to look at the Pasionaria. Her eyes were fixed on the glorious creation of chrome and paint, and we all held our breath for a moment: the queen, we thought, was about to descend from her pedestal and become, once again, a human being like the rest of us. Her face, which had paled at this unexpected stroke, began to redden, her eyes glittered, her lips trembled.

"Now at last," we all thought, "she's going to cry out, she's going to hop and skip!"

But her face resumed its normal color, her eyes lost their glitter.

"It's a Legnano," the Pasionaria observed distantly, as she sat down again. "Does it have a bell?"

Albertino trilled the bell.

"All right," said the Pasionaria.

It was something, but it wasn't even the shadow of what we had hoped for.

Margherita was furious.

"If she were my daughter," she whispered fiercely, "I know what I'd do with her!"

"But she *is* your daughter, Margherita," I said.

"No," replied Margherita, "she's not our daughter today —today she belongs to some other world."

By now the flow of gifts was definitely exhausted. The Pasionaria, sitting in a leather armchair, continued to grant a few words to the people around her, a few short words that seemed to have come all the way down from the eighteenth floor, words that had been left up there in space and fluttered down lightly, like dead leaves.

Margherita's resentment grew.

"Pretty soon," she whispered in my ear, "if we want an audience with her, we'll have to request it on official paper. Would you like to see me lift her train and give her a good spanking?"

"I would indeed," I said, fascinated.

But I saw nothing of the sort. Margherita did indeed go to the Pasionaria, and with light fingers touched the long gown—but only to straighten it. The Pasionaria thanked her with a slight inclination of the head, and Margherita blushed with pleasure.

That's how things stood when there was another ring at the gate, and Albertino ran to open it. He returned highly excited, dragging behind him another box about the size of that of the bicycle. The Pasionaria deigned to turn her head. She made it clear that by now this matter of the gifts was beginning to bore her. However, one couldn't ignore the new box entirely.

Albertino had the energy and enthusiasm of a storming party: the wooden crate was quickly broken open, the paper wrapping torn away. There appeared then the strangest-looking object in the world: bright green with yellow trim.

We hadn't the slightest idea what it was. I lifted the singular machine up out of the litter in which it lay and carried it over to the light.

"What on earth is it?" asked Margherita.

"A corking machine," I replied. "But I can't imagine who would make a little girl a gift of a machine that puts corks into bottles."

"A lot of those friends of yours," said Margherita in a disgusted voice, "are only too ready for jokes. It must have been Brogetto. Or else that idiot Gigi."

"Or maybe even Signor Carletto," added Albertino.

Margherita was indignant.

"It's all very well," she cried, "for grown-ups to play jokes among themselves. But to play a joke on a little girl on the day of her First Communion is the work of an ill-bred moron. The sins of the fathers should not be visited on innocent children."

There was general agreement as Margherita went to the telephone. She came back in a frenzy.

"Gigi and Brogetto swear they didn't do it," she said. "It must have been Carletto. But he wasn't home."

"I'm here," said Carletto. "I swear I didn't do it—I gave her the little sewing basket."

"But *somebody* did it," cried Margherita.

She drew us all into a corner and in an agitated voice went on: "Do something, for the love of God! Try to take her mind off it. Tell her it was a mistake. She's a highly sensitive little girl. Whoever played this ghastly trick— and I have no doubt it was somebody her father associates with politically—it can leave a terrible scar on the child's mind. It's the kind of thing that can poison her forever! Come, quick, we must do something!"

We went to do something, but it was too late. The Pasionaria was standing beside the offending machine, gazing gravely at it. I went to her. She raised her eyes. She looked up at me. I felt my heart being wrung. Everyone was silent and sad, for we read something ineffably sad in the eyes of the child.

"Why?" asked the Pasionaria, in a small, plaintive voice.

I didn't know what to say.

"Why what?" I stammered.

"Why," she said, "does it have this iron wire with the stamped lead thing?"

"That's the seal of guaranty," I explained. "That means that after the machine was examined, nobody has lifted the lever."

The Pasionaria went on staring at the machine.

"How does it work?" she asked.

I tore off the wire and the seal.

"You lift this lever, you put a cork in here, you pull down the lever, and the cork goes into the bottle."

"You mean a big cork like that goes into the tiny little opening of the bottle?" The Pasionaria was astonished. "I'd like to see it work."

I rummaged through the kitchen-table drawer and found some new corks. I moistened them with olive oil and brought them, along with some empty bottles, into the living room. I put the bottle in place, then the cork, then pressed down on the lever.

Until that moment the Pasionaria had maintained her attitude of a woman who is not of this world. But when she saw the cork enter the neck of the bottle, she was visibly, and deeply, stirred. She wanted me to repeat the operation with another bottle.

"Is it hard?" she asked, much moved.

"On the contrary," I replied, "it's very easy." I explained how the machine worked.

The Pasionaria put in the third cork. "Again!" she cried, enthusiastically.

I sent out for five hundred corks from a nearby shop, and from the cellar I had two hundred bottles brought up that I was keeping to return to the wine merchant.

Margherita went to the Pasionaria. "Let me at least take off your gown," she said.

"No, no!" cried the Pasionaria. "Please! I've got work to do!" She began to cork the bottles.

With the disappearance of each cork into a bottle, her excitement mounted, and at the twentieth she began to laugh and shout. Albertino and the other children organized a cork detail and helped with the work, but the management remained in the hands of the Pasionaria.

Then the telephone rang.

"It's the messenger who brought the machine," said Margherita. "He says he made a mistake and is coming to take it away, he's bringing another package with what he thinks is a tricycle or something like that."

I took the phone.

"No," I told him, "leave things as they are. If the man who was supposed to get the machine doesn't want the tricycle, tell him I'll send him another machine exactly like this tomorrow."

A half hour later, a very excited man was on the phone.

"That machine is mine!" he shouted. "I ordered it, and I want it!"

"You'll get one just like it," I told him. "Or, if you'd rather, I'll pay you for this one at once. I'm willing to pay more than it cost—it's for my little girl, who's just made her First Communion."

The man shouted even louder. "What's a First Communion got to do with a bottle-capping machine? I'm going to denounce you for embezzlement of property!"

Margherita grabbed the telephone from my hands. "Have you no shame?" she cried in a voice quivering with emotion. "Trying to disrupt a mystical experience! If you are an atheist or an anarchist, why pick on our house for your anticlerical demonstrations?"

Margherita listened for a few moments, then put down the receiver.

"What did he tell you?" I asked.

"Oh, he told me he was a parish priest," she replied simply. "He calmed down, of course. He realized his position was untenable."

The corking operation went on until late afternoon. We found that every bottle in the house had been corked—even my bottle of India ink. I don't know how they managed it, but they even corked the barrels of my fowling iron.

That night, before going to bed, I glanced into the Pasionaria's camp site. She was sleeping soundly. At the foot of her bed was the corking machine, and on the corking machine lay her gown of white lace.

THE "M" LEAGUE

I fell off my motorcycle, which was disagreeable, but most disagreeable of all was the fact that I tore my brown corduroy jacket irreparably.

"Nothing to it," I said, "but to have a new jacket made. As soon as I get to Milan tomorrow, I'll buy the material and call the tailor."

Margherita spoke up with the full force of her authority.

"Leave it to me!" she said. "I'll call now. That way, when you get to Milan, it will all be ready and you won't make a mess of things, as you usually do. Just wait for the tailor to come and take your measurements. We'll let him know, too."

When Margherita says we, I know it means she's going to make use of the famous and well-organized Margherita League.

I thought no more about it and the next morning left peacefully for Milan.

At 10:30 Signora Maria telephoned me. She sounded troubled.

"It's a big mess," she said, "and Marcellina has finally broken it off."

I did not know who Marcellina was, nor could I imagine what she had broken off, but Signora Maria soon enlightened me.

"And it wasn't Marcella's fault," she said. "Luigi has behaved very badly, saying that Ernesta was right."

"I'm afraid I don't understand," I murmured.

"You just ask your wife, she'll understand. And tell her for the time being we'll have to wait until we find another way. Besides, you don't need the corduroy jacket right away, do you?"

Here, at last, was something I could understand.

"No, of course not," I said, "the corduroy jacket isn't terribly urgent. But what has Marcella got to do with it, and Ernesta, and Luigi?"

Signora Maria laughed.

"That's easy!" she cried. "Luigi's the one who sells the corduroy, and now we can't use Marcellina any more to get the special discount, because she's broken off relations with Luigi, so obviously we'll have to find some other way to do it. You just tell your wife I'm working on it."

Half an hour later there was a ring at the door. When I went down to open it, I found a girl there who was unknown to me.

"I'm Cesarina's friend," she said. "Cesarina told me to come around to see if the quality was all right."

I spread out my hands; the girl realized I had no idea what she was talking about.

"The jacket's Cesarina's, but she lent it to me, so that's why I came. Here, look."

The jacket was of green wool, and while I appreciated the softness of the material, I told her that what I wanted was a jacket of brown corduroy.

The girl stood lost in thought for a moment, then said it was all very peculiar.

"Probably what happened," she went on, "is that Giulietta didn't explain it very well when she called Cesarina. Or more likely still, it was Antonia who gave Giulietta the wrong information because I can assure you Cesarina has never had jackets of brown corduroy."

I thanked the girl and apologized for having unwittingly caused her so much trouble.

I had no sooner got back to work than the tailor arrived. He took my measurements, then asked for the material.

"Signora Maria," he said, "told me she was going to send it over."

"We have to wait," I said, "because Marcella has broken off with Luigi. Luigi has behaved very badly."

"The Luigi who sells the material?"

"That's the one. Believe it or not, he took Ernesta's side."

"Disgraceful!" cried the tailor. "I know what kind of girl Ernesta is."

The tailor left, and ten minutes later a boy was at the door.

"I'm the carpenter," he said. "Signora Ferretti sent me."

I told him he must have made a mistake, and he started to leave, mumbling angrily, when I realized he was wearing a jacket of brown corduroy, so I called him back.

"Would you mind telling me," I asked, "where you bought that material?"

"I don't know. My sister buys all my clothes."

I had just closed the door behind him when the telephone rang.

"In a little while," said Signora Maria, "there'll be a carpenter coming to see you. Give him some small job to do, and meanwhile take a look at his jacket and let me know if you like the material."

"I like it fine," I said. "He was here two minutes ago."

"Then everything's in order!" cried Signora Maria cheerfully. "We've found another way. You'll get it this evening."

That was all I wanted to know, and I thanked the good Lord that the affair was finally ended.

Ten minutes later, however, the phone rang again. It was a man this time, and he sounded very angry.

"I don't have the pleasure," he said, "of knowing you personally, although I follow your work and think very highly of it, and so I was very sorry to hear that you had said such unpleasant things about me. . . . I beg your pardon, will you let me go on? I know perfectly well that someone has been telling you lies about me, and I would like you to realize that I have always behaved correctly with Marcella and that the story about Ernesta is a complete invention on somebody's part. Do you honestly believe I could behave that way with a woman like Ernesta?"

"Certainly not!" I cried. "I know what kind of girl Ernesta is. Therefore—"

"Therefore all's well that ends well," Luigi interrupted, for it was indeed Luigi, the Luigi that sells the material.

We said goodbye in a friendly fashion, I put down the receiver, and went to open the door, for there had been a ring at the bell.

The tailor came in with a package. He unwrapped it and showed me, much surprised, a length of material for shirts.

"I can't make you a brown corduroy jacket out of blue poplin," he said.

I could not but agree with him and assured him I had no idea how the blue poplin had got into the picture.

"Signora Maria sent it to me," he cried, "saying it was for the brown corduroy jacket!"

As fate would have it, Signora Maria herself telephoned me at that very moment.

"Everything's all right again!" she announced. "Marcella has made up with Luigi. Therefore, we go back to regular channels. The tailor will get the material tonight."

"Fine, fine!" I cried. "But the tailor is here right now with a length of poplin—"

"Don't worry about that," she said. "By the time I heard about the reconciliation, I'd already ordered the corduroy somewhere else, and since I didn't want to embarrass Signora Lucia I changed the order. Your wife told me you need some shirts too!"

I took the poplin and asked the tailor to wait, in peace and in his own house, for the arrival of the corduroy. The tailor left, and the telephone rang. It was a young woman's voice, and she sounded upset.

"I would like to know," she cried, "how you have the nerve to speak that way about me!"

I said there must be a mistake; I had no idea what she meant.

"You know very well what I mean!" she replied. "My name is Ernesta, and you spoke against me to Luigi. His friend Francesca told me, she got it from that creature Marcella!"

I begged her to be calm.

"I assure you," I said, "that it's all a mistake. I don't know anybody and I haven't spoken ill of anybody."

She calmed down, and I thought the whole thing was finished at last, when, just as I was beginning lunch, Signora Maria telephoned.

"It's all off," she told me. "Marcella has had another quarrel with Luigi. We'll have to try the other way again."

Then Luigi called; he was very angry.

"Would you mind repeating to me," he said, "exactly what you told that nut Ernesta?"

"I only said I don't know anybody and I haven't spoken ill of anybody."

"Would you care to deny that you told me you know Ernesta very well and you know exactly what kind of girl she is?"

"All I did was to repeat, very stupidly, a remark made by Nicola, my tailor."

Then all went back to normal and stayed normal until seven o'clock that evening. At seven o'clock the tailor arrived.

"You've got me into trouble," he said sadly. "The remark I made about Ernesta, I made in confidence. You shouldn't have gone and repeated it all around."

I tried to console the poor unhappy tailor, and swore I would never answer the telephone again.

It rang at least six different times between then and midnight. The next day it rang twenty times. As I didn't answer it, I had no more news of the brown corduroy jacket. The day after, however, Signora Maria arrived in person.

"There must be something wrong with your telephone," she said. "Anyway, the way things stand now—"

"I don't want to know!" I cried. "Tell my wife about it!"

"All right, I'll write her. Meanwhile, here's the material for your jacket." She handed me a package, and when I unwrapped it I saw it contained a length of blue material with white stripes.

"That's fine," I said, "it's exactly what I wanted. And give my best wishes to Luigi and Marcella."

Signora Maria shook her head.

"Very bad," she said, "very bad. Do you remember that carpenter who came here, sent by Signora Ferretti?"

"Yes."

"Well, Marcella has left Luigi and has got engaged to him. So when you need any material just call me because I've struck up a friendship with the carpenter's sister, and that channel is always open."

When I got back to the country, Margherita asked me if everything had gone all right.

"Perfectly," I replied. "It worked like a charm."

"You see?" Margherita cried. "It's best to leave things like that to us women. You men can complicate even the simplest matters."

A PROFESSION FOR PAPA

That evening after supper I said to the Pasionaria: "The bag!"

The Pasionaria gave me a look, then turned to Margherita: "Papa wants the hot-water bag. Where is it?"

I broke in firmly: "I didn't ask for the hot-water bag. I want to see your school bag."

The Pasionaria appeared to be astonished.

"My school bag?" she repeated. "What do you want with that?"

"I want to see what you're doing at school."

With infinite slowness, the Pasionaria moved over toward the corner where she kept her magazines.

"If everybody," she muttered, "minded their own business, we'd all be a lot better off . . . "

Once I had the bag, I began to leaf through the exercise books. What particularly interested me was the composition book, and it was there. Indeed, I found something that disturbed me deeply:

"THEME: Your parents. Describe their life, character, and work.

"TREATMENT: My parents are nice people. Mama is the goddess of the hearth and she stands over our gas stove cooking delicious food that looks very pretty on the table, but I like cold meat and potato salad better. Mama is always telling us to be neat and clean because otherwise people will say we look like gypsies.

"My papa is the support of the family and works very hard because he is always going around the house hammering in nails for pictures, tightening water faucets, regulating the gas heater, or else supervising the builders and the carpenter.

"Sometimes my papa washes the car and then he dries it with a piece of leather. He also puts water in the radiator and makes sure the motor has enough gas.

"My papa can also typewrite in both black and red. He likes to read and he reads a lot of newspapers.

"He drives to Milan every week and then he comes back and my mama is happy because the electric light has to be fixed or the furnace needs more gas or the big clock has to be wound or something.

"In character my parents are bad-tempered but they are good people and I like them fairly well and even when they annoy me I always forgive them."

After I'd read the composition, I turned to the Pasionaria.

"If I understand you correctly," I said, "your father's work consists in hanging pictures, winding the clock, and driving to Milan. Then where do I get the money that you and I live on?"

The Pasionaria shrugged. "I," she said, "never mix in other people's affairs."

"A wise principle!" I cried. "However, a daughter ought at the very least to know what her father's profession is. Don't you know that, in addition to fixing the water tap in the bathroom and the fuse box, I also write articles for newspapers, and books?"

"Of course I *know*," said the Pasionaria. "But that's not a profession like a carpenter or a doctor or an engineer or a lawyer."

"What is it, then?" I cried.

"Oh, it's just something. Anybody can write. But if a man isn't a doctor, he can't cut off somebody's leg."

I grew indignant. "In that case, your father's just a nobody without a profession?"

The Pasionaria was not much affected by my outburst.

"A profession," she said, "is when somebody does something people need. If people need clothes they call the tailor, if they need medicine they call the doctor, if they need a table made they call the carpenter. Those are professions. But nobody calls in a writer because they need a story to make them laugh or cry."

"But you," I cried, "you read the stories in your books and magazines!"

"That doesn't mean anything," said the Pasionaria. "There are children who don't read stories and nothing happens to them. But if a child has shoes that need fixing and there's no shoemaker to do it, then she has to go around barefoot. Or if a man has to go to court and he hasn't got a lawyer, he ends up in jail."

I could hardly undertake to enter into the long discussion with the Pasionaria that the case called for.

In any event, Margherita broke in at that point.

"There you are," she murmured. "How many times have I said to you, 'Take your examinations, Giovannino, get your degree, then you'd have a profession'? You get no

sympathy from me when your children say you haven't
got a profession."

"But if Papa wanted," said Albertino to Margherita, "he
could still take his examinations and get a degree."

"Too late!" replied Margherita. "He'd have to begin all
over again—he doesn't remember a thing any more.
Haven't you noticed how he can't make head or tail out of
even Latin or mathematics when you ask him for help?"

Here the Pasionaria let her voice be heard.

"Even if he can't take a degree," she said, "he could at
least find something to do. He could open a shop, for
instance. You don't need a diploma to be a shopkeeper."

Margherita laughed.

"Go into business?" she cried. "Don't even think about
it—if he opened a store, it would fail in two weeks."

"He could be a traveling salesman," Albertino suggested.

"He's too unrealistic," Margherita declared. "He's not
made for any kind of business."

"He could be a truck driver!" cried the Pasionaria. "He
has a license and he knows how to drive."

Margherita shook her head.

"That's hard work," she said. "He's old now, he's worn
out, his eyes are always tired."

The Pasionaria looked at me with sympathy.

"Then there's nothing he can do any more," she said
sadly. "Poor old thing."

Margherita shook her head.

"Nothing at all," she said. "Just go on living from hand
to mouth as he always has. Like a bird in a tree! As
disorganized and absent-minded as the day I met him."

"If he was disorganized and absent-minded," the Pasionaria asked, "why did you marry him?"

Margherita spread her hands.

"Maybe," she replied, "because I was even more absent-minded."

The Pasionaria seemed much impressed by this maternal revelation. She went off to put her school bag in order.

I noticed that before she put her composition book back, she wrote something in it, and after everybody had gone to bed, I took it out and found that the treatment of her theme had been somewhat enlarged:

"My papa writes for newspapers but his profession is truck driver. My mama is also a truck driver, and when my papa has to make a long trip, my mama drives while her husband rests on the berth in the cabin of the truck. Our truck is a diesel Fiat, latest model. It is very beautiful and on the front is written in big letters: 'God Save Us.'"

So the Pasionaria had overcome all obstacles and promoted me to truck driver; and out of consideration for my infirmities, to make the work easier, she had put Margherita beside me, as assistant truck driver.

Now I too had a profession.

I put out the light and joined the assistant truck driver, who was sleeping on the berth in the cabin of the truck.

Soon I was speeding along the empty roads of sleep.

THE MILANESE FACE

"This morning," said Margherita, "there was a farmer on a motorcycle who came. He said he wanted to do your bust."

There is nothing very strange about a farmer riding a motorcycle; what is strange is that, once he got here, he wanted to do a bust.

"Did he say what his name was?" I asked.

"No," said Margherita. "He got off the motorcycle, he came in, he said, 'Is the guy with the mustache here?' I told him no. Then he said, 'Tell him I'm expecting him—I want to do his bust.' Then he got back on his motorcycle and that was the end of him."

"He didn't say anything else?"

"Nothing."

"How was he dressed?"

"Leather overalls, leather gauntlets, leather helmet, and goggles."

The thing kept getting less comprehensible.

"Margherita, did he have anything on the back of the motorcycle? Like spades or hoes or harrows or plows, any kind of farm equipment?"

"All he had was a camera slung over his shoulder."

I lost all patience.

"Somebody came here on a motorcycle," I cried,

"dressed as an aviator, with a camera over his shoulders! And who is he? A farmer! May I ask, Margherita, how you knew he was a farmer?"

Margherita did not fly off the handle.

"By his face," she replied quietly. "After he took his goggles off, I recognized that farmer who came to see you once in Milan, five or six years ago, and you talked all day about manure and farms and cattle and stables and so on. You know who I mean?"

"No."

"Well, he's the same farmer who came today to tell you he's expecting you because he wants to do your bust."

Then light dawned.

"I know who he is now!" I cried. "He's not a farmer, even though he dresses like an aviator and rides a motorcycle. He's a sculptor—and that's why he wants to do a bust of me."

"He's a farmer," Margherita declared. "I know he's a farmer because he wrote you once and on the back of the envelope was his occupation in big letters."

There was something in what she said, for those were the days when the sculptor Froni had his letterpaper imprinted: "Froni—Farmer—Fidenza," and all he talked about was farming.

"It seems he's changed occupations again," I said, "and now he's gone back to his own."

In addition to being an old friend, Froni was, and still is, one of the very few sculptors in the world who are really sculptors. I went to his house the next morning.

He was in his studio, working on a head. He didn't turn when I said hello to him.

"Don't move, Giovannino!" he cried excitedly. "Stay where you are! Let me get the clay ready. I don't want to weaken the first impression. When I tell you, go and sit on that stool and look at the window catch. Then I'll turn and look at you and begin to work you right away in the clay. Five minutes later I'll throw you out, and in two months I'll finish the bust. But it's the first impression that counts and I've got to catch it in its full intensity."

I said I would obey instructions.

"Giovannino," cried the sculptor as he prepared a slab of clay on a stand, "I've been thinking about doing you for a year. I'm convinced I'll do something really good— yours is the face I need right now. All right! Go and sit on that stool and face the window."

I went to sit on the stool and face the window.

The sculptor turned and fixed his eyes on me.

I held my breath so as not to weaken the intensity of the first impression, but almost at once I heard Froni's voice, and it was a completely different voice from that of a moment ago.

"No," he said, "it won't work. It isn't you."

The disappointment I heard in his voice saddened me.

"I'm sorry," I stammered. "Maybe the light—"

"No!" he shook his head. "It just isn't you. When I saw you in Milan five years ago, you didn't look like this. You had a face that said something then—your hair fell over your forehead, you had bags under your eyes, there were deep lines around your mouth. . . . Now you're all changed. You've got a placid face—the face of a man who's doing all right, who eats and drinks in peace without worrying about anything, the face—"

"The face of a moron," I said, "in other words."

"No. Just a face that isn't very interesting."

I felt a sense of guilt.

"Well, I slept a lot last night," I said. "And this morning, before I came here, I had my hair cut. The last time you saw me, I was dead tired, I hadn't slept for two nights, I hadn't combed my hair, I had a stomach ache—"

"Giovannino, you shouldn't have come this morning."

"How could I tell what kind of face you wanted?"

"I want that other face! The one that interests me. Next time, come when you're tired, when you haven't combed your hair or shaved, when you have bags under your eyes, when you've been smoking too much. When, in a word, you have a *presentable* face! I want to do your portrait, but first I've got to have that other face."

He spoke on and on about how eager he was to get going on my portrait, and soon he was carried away by his enthusiasm.

I was convinced, by the time I left, that if I didn't resume my Milanese face I'd be guilty of the dirtiest trick anybody ever played.

A month later I went back.

"You're disgusting, Giovannino," Margherita had said to me that morning, as she looked at my face and the immediate surroundings.

So instead of going to the barber's I went to Froni's.

He leapt with joy when he saw me.

"Stay there, stay there, Giovannino!" he cried. "Don't move!" Feverishly he began to slap pieces of clay onto the stand. "Don't move, we've got it now!"

I turned off the motor and waited, sitting on the stool, looking at the window.

He worked on the clay for about a quarter of an hour,

and every once in a while he sobbed, "Don't move, I've got it. I've got it now, don't move!"

Then suddenly he roared out, "No!"

"I haven't got it," he went on, between clenched teeth. "It's all wrong. It looked like you, it looked like the Milanese face. But it's not you and it isn't that face."

I tried to persuade him he was wrong. I was dead tired because I hadn't slept for two nights, my eyes were bleary, I hadn't shaved or cut my hair or even combed it.

"I'm just as I was," I concluded, "except I'm five years older. And except for the stomach ache, which I don't have today. But that can't be very important—"

"Not important?" he cried. "Don't you know what a stomach ache means?"

I knew very well, all too well, in fact—for stomach aches had poisoned my life for nearly fifteen years.

I nodded. "But you're not going to try to tell me," I said, "that my face comes from a stomach ache?"

"I'm not trying to tell you anything! I'm only telling you that when you come next time, have a stomach ache. I want your real face!"

Well, it was no longer a question of friendship, it was a case of conscience. Since he was sure my portrait would be a masterpiece, my clear duty was to make a few sacrifices out of love of the artist and the art that was in him. So I made a few sacrifices and began to eat salami and sausages and fried stuff and peppers and anchovies— all the things, in other words, that I loved the most and that made me suffer the most.

I continued this hellish diet for a month, but clearly fate was against me and, therefore, against art: I didn't even have a touch of heartburn. Then, at last, I woke up one morning with the grandfather of all stomach aches. I didn't even wash. I dressed any old way, jumped into the car, and started off for Fidenza. All the while I concentrated on my stomach ache, and it's well known that if you have a stomach ache there's nothing worse for it than to think about stomach aches.

Of course I drove badly, which was how I almost got smashed to bits by a trailer truck on a bad part of the road. I swerved and got the car back onto the road with a dexterity I didn't know I possessed. The bumper wasn't even scratched, but for a moment I lost control of my stomach ache, and when I got control again, it was gone.

I returned home disconsolate.

Days went by, and weeks, and one evening Froni turned up.

"Well?" he said.

I spread my hands.

"If you don't want me to do your portrait," he cried bitterly, "just tell me! But don't forget this is the first favor I've ever asked of you. . . ."

I protested; I described all I'd been doing to get a stomach ache. I even called in Margherita as a witness: "Tell him what kind of junk I've been eating."

Margherita looked at the sculptor with hatred in her eyes.

"It would have been better," she said coldly, "if you'd stayed a farmer. I tell you, if he goes on this way for another month, you'll have to do a bust of him for the cemetery! Look at him! Look what you've brought him to! He never goes to the barber, he sleeps in his clothes, he hardly ever washes—he's a disgrace to the house! Does it have to be him you do a portrait of?"

The sculptor spread his hands.

"It has to be him!" he cried. "Oh, he was a wonder when I saw him that time in Milan!"

Margherita made no more objections. She realized that he wanted to do my portrait not out of spite but because his art required it of him.

"Well," she said with a sigh, "it will be as God wills. Men pass but art remains. Let's just hope it doesn't come too late."

I went on working toward the glory of art, eating and drinking things that would have given a rhinoceros a bellyache.

But they gave none to me. I had just about given up all hope when one night at about two o'clock I woke up with such pains in the stomach as I had never had before.

"Margherita!" I cried. "I've got it!"

"Thank God," breathed Margherita.

I didn't even dress. I threw my overcoat over me, got the car out of the garage, and hurtled into the dark night.

As I flew over the road, my stomach ache, instead of going away, as I feared it might, actually got worse. It was fantastic!

I got to Froni's house, which was deep in the country.

I threw pebbles at the window until I woke him up. He opened the door for me, and I ran immediately into the studio and sat down on the stool facing the window.

"Hurry up!" I cried. "I've got it! If you don't see the Milanese face now, you'll never see it. I've got a stomach ache that's killing me!"

"So have I," said Froni drearily. "Unless I find some bicarbonate of soda, I won't be able to move a finger."

He shuddered with pain.

It is not easy to find bicarbonate of soda at three in the morning. We got into the car and finally located some, around six, at Parma.

When an hour later I dropped him off at his house, Froni looked at me and shook his head sadly.

"You had a marvelous face last night," he said, "the real Milanese face. But now. . . ."

He sighed deeply.

"Giovannino," he said, "a true friend would not have taken the bicarbonate. He would have done without. . . . I'm the only one who should have had it!"

Humbly, I headed home. When Margherita saw me, she understood at once.

"Did it go wrong again?"

"Wrong."

"You must have faith, Giovannino. Art is a stern mistress. But don't be discouraged—you'll recover the Milanese face. You *must* recover it! Because, you know, he's right, that man: it's your true face. An interesting face. When you're feeling well, you have the face—I don't know quite how to put it—the face—"

"Of a moron," I said. I knew how to put it.

THE DELEGATE

I was in the kitchen. Albertino and the Pasionaria marched in, their flanks protected, and I realized I now had to face mass action.

At a safe distance, the platoon halted. After a slight hesitation, the Pasionaria detached herself from the ranks and marched directly on the objective.

I pretended to be unaware of the maneuver. "What do you want?" I asked.

"Me? Nothing. I'm here as a delegate."

"A delegate? What does that mean?"

"That means I'm here to speak on behalf of all the others."

"All what others?"

She indicated Albertino, who was still standing at attention.

"Him. And me when I'm with him."

I began to laugh.

"Who are you when you're not with him?" I asked. "What's the difference between you when you're with your brother and you when you're three yards away from him, as you are now?"

"The difference is that now I'm a delegate, and so I haven't come to tell you what I want myself but what I've been ordered to tell you by all the others."

The Pasionaria is quick-witted and on the ball. She

never woolgathers, so when she says something that sounds a bit odd, that's the time to pay the most careful attention to her words.

The distinction she had just made seemed, on consideration, subtle but precise: the fact that she was now standing in front of me, and not on her brother's flank, made no effective change in the situation. The attacking power of the ranks standing at attention was undiminished, for at Albertino's side stood the Pasionaria who had decided, along with Albertino, to send the same Pasionaria forward as a delegate. And this Pasionaria came as a delegate to speak not in her own name and her brother's but in the name of a federation composed of herself and her brother. There were, therefore, one Albertino and two Pasionarias.

Today's child—I think there can be no doubt of it— looks at the world very differently from yesterday's. The latter would have said, "I am speaking for myself and my brother." But the Pasionaria said, "I am speaking as a delegate for the entire company."

"Very well then," I said to the delegate. "What do they want of me?"

"They want to know if they can have an advance."

Margherita, who had just come into the kitchen, shared my surprise.

"An advance?" she cried. "Why? Have you suddenly become civil service workers, or something?"

The Pasionaria made no reply. She did an about-face and retreated to confer with the company.

When she resumed the conference, she said to Margherita, "I'm speaking to him, not to you. You don't have anything to do with the question of the advance."

I asked Margherita not to interrupt the negotiations in

progress between the employer and the employees. I then turning to the delegate.

"You would like an advance?" I said. "Very well, the subject is open for discussion. But it's a question of an advance on what?"

"It's a question of an advance on the inheritance."

Margherita started.

"Heartless wretches!" she shrieked. "Do you want to kill your father off? Shame on both of you!"

"We don't want to kill anybody off," replied the Pasionaria firmly. "All we're asking is, can we have an advance on our inheritance? An inheritance exists, after all, even if somebody lives a thousand years."

It occured to me that the Pasionaria was somewhat confused on the subject of inheritances.

"No," I told her, "an inheritance doesn't come into existence until the decease of the person who leaves his worldly goods to his heirs. The heir is the person who receives the goods of the deceased."

The Pasionaria's expression was so perplexed, I tried to explain the concept more clearly: "To say that an inheritance exists even if the person lives a thousand years is like saying widowhood exists even if the husband and wife live a thousand years. In other words, as long as I'm alive, do you think your mother can call herself a widow?"

The Pasionaria looked questioningly at Margherita, who indicated that the answer was no.

"No," said the Pasionaria.

"And as long as I'm alive," I went on, "do you think you two can call yourselves my orphans?"

"As far as I'm concerned," said the Pasionaria, "no. I can't speak for the others."

She turned to look at Albertino, who shook his head.

"The others also say no," she said.

I charged on. "Well, then, as long as I'm alive, your mother can't say she's my widow and you can't say you're my orphans, so how can you possibly say you're my heirs?"

The Pasionaria did not feel she could assume the responsibility for so binding an answer. She went to confer with Albertino, then declared: "They say they can. Even if somebody lives a thousand years, there's still an inheritance."

"The children are right," said Margherita. "An inheritance is not a contingent factor, it's absolute. Widowhood is something else again, it only occurs when the husband dies. It's like baldness—if a woman loses her husband, she becomes a widow, and if she loses her hair, she becomes bald. Inheritance, on the other hand, is a factor that doesn't depend on any other factors. Giovannino, if you— God forbid!—were to die this minute, wouldn't your children inherit?"

"Certainly."

"All right. But you didn't die this minute, so your children didn't inherit anything. Yet the inheritance exists, because if you had died this minute, they—as you've already admitted—would inherit."

"Correct!" said the Pasionaria.

"Mama's right," said Albertino, who apparently had also been sent in as a delegate.

"No," I said, "your mother's wrong. An inheritance constitutes the goods that a man, when he dies, leaves to his children or his family. But as long as that man's alive, no one can speak with any certainty of an inheritance—

maybe today he's worth ten million but when he dies he doesn't have a penny. A lot of men are rich at eighty and die at eighty-three penniless. So how can you speak of an 'advance on your inheritance' if nobody on earth can say whether I'll leave you anything when I move on to the next world?"

The Pasionaria was not convinced.

"But you just said if you were to die now, you'd leave all your stuff to us. Therefore, there *is* an inheritance."

"Only if I die this second. But I don't intend to die this second just to do you a favor! I'll die when it pleases God—and until that time, there is no inheritance, there is only my estate. My estate is something I possess today and tomorrow may not."

The squadron withdrew, and a short while later the delegate returned.

"They would like," said the Pasionaria, "to have an advance on the estate."

"How clever they are, Giovannino," said Margherita with a proud smile. "How quickly they grasped the concept!"

"They've grasped nothing!" I cried. At this, the second delegate joined the first. "An advance," I went on, "is money granted today against a compensation which is due tomorrow. If someone is working for me, he can ask me for money in anticipation of what I'm going to owe him. But nobody can ask me for money in anticipation of what I don't owe him. My estate is mine!"

"All right, but don't you think you ought to leave your children something? Don't you *owe* them that? And if so, why can't they ask you for an advance on it?"

"This is too much!" I shouted. "So we're back again on the inheritance jag!"

"No, we're not," declared the Pasionaria. "There's no inheritance until somebody dies and then you see whether he's left you something or not. But if there's an estate, you can ask for an advance on it."

I banged my fist on the table.

"No, no, no!" I cried. "If I grant you an advance on my present estate, I am conceding the fact that that estate is yours and so bind myself morally to preserve it intact till the end of my days. But I don't owe you anything, and I intend to administer my estate as I like and as I please. And I'm not obliged to leave you anything. On the contrary! I'm grateful to my parents chiefly for two things: they brought me into the world and they gave me the opportunity to earn my own living since I was a young boy. *The man who doesn't work doesn't eat!* You can write those seven words on the walls of your room, in all your books, in your brain itself—it's the way of life of all men worthy of the name!"

The Pasionaria gave Albertino a look, then turned back to me.

"Very well," she said, "tomorrow we'll go out and get work on a construction gang."

With some people, there's just no point in going on, better to let the thing drop.

"Congratulations," I said. "In that case, you can ask for an advance from the foreman. I don't give advances to people I don't owe anything to. My money, the money I earn, I give to people who work for me, or to unfortunate people who can't find work."

They left without daring to look at me again.

"They're sensitive children," said Margherita. "You were too mordant with them."

"Margherita," I said, "yesterday I heard you use the word 'illation,' today 'mordant.' Aren't ordinary words any use to you to express your thoughts? Are you headed in the direction of intellectualism?"

"No," she replied placidly, "but now and then I like to pause for a moment to pick some exotic flower out of the word garden, to dress an old thought in a new color."

"Then you must be aware that sometimes we must take energetic, even cruel measures with the children. We must wake them now and then to the gelid reality of life."

"But you humiliated them. That's not right."

The Pasionaria returned.

"We," she said, "are two unemployed construction workers. If you could see your way clear to helping us. . . ."

I saw my way clear. It was rather expensive, too, because they apparently needed an awful lot of things.

But the principle had been upheld.

THE VILLAGE OF
DON CAMILLO

We drove for a long time over country roads full of rocks
and holes. When we finally got to the village, we parked
the car in the square.

Mario, the friend who was with us, got out of the car
along with Albertino.

"Wait for me here," he said. "If this guy's at home, I'll
try to get it over with in a quarter of an hour. Meanwhile
you can amuse yourselves by looking around you."

There wasn't much to look at. We were in one of those
familiar towns lost in the great plain beside the river:
little red, yellow, and blue houses; narrow, winding
streets; four little shops under the portico in the square.
The usual boredom, the usual sun.

I suggested a beer.

"Fine with me," said the Pasionaria.

"Not me," Margherita declared. "I'd rather stay in the
car. I don't trust them here."

I began to laugh.

"Margherita," I said, "this is a civilized place. There
aren't any highway robbers here."

"It's not a question of civilization or highway robbers—
it's a question of politics. This is the reddest town in the
plain. In the last elections everyone voted Communist
except the priest. I read about it in the paper."

"So what? Drinking a beer isn't holding an anti-Communist meeting, is it?"

"I'm not afraid of the Communists," declared the Pasionaria.

"Nor am I," said Margherita. "Unless you provoke them, Communists behave just like everybody else."

"Well, who intends to provoke them?" I asked, rather annoyed.

"It's not the intention that counts, it's your face. Your face is a living provocation. It's a well-known, unmistakable face, and even if they've never seen you in person, they'd know you, and they know what you are."

"And what am I, according to you?"

"According to me, you're the disgrace of the family. According to them, you're the fellow who's been heaping insults on them week after week, year after year, making fun of them and drawing nasty cartoons of them."

"What's that got to do with it? I'm not going to write an article, I'm going to drink a beer."

"You can't erase the past with a beer! The man who offers an insult writes it in sand, but for the man who receives it it's chiseled in bronze."

"Do as you like," I said. "I am going to have something to drink."

"Would you really leave two poor women here alone and unprotected? Giovannino, you're very thoughtless."

"I get it," grumbled the Pasionaria. "I'll go, that way there'll only be one woman alone, protected by a mustache."

Margherita gave a shriek of horror.

"Giovannino, you wouldn't let her go alone!"

"No, Margherita," I replied, "I wouldn't let her go alone. The trouble is, she's already gone."

The Pasionaria was trotting over toward the portico. When she reached it, she turned, stuck her tongue out at me, and disappeared.

"The sins of the fathers!" cried Margherita. "Oh, Giovannino, if anything happens to that poor little thing, I don't know what I'll do."

"Neither do I." I got my newspaper out of the glove compartment and was soon far from my immediate surroundings.

But not for long.

"Giovannino!" cried Margherita. "Look!"

I looked, and saw five or six people standing together under one of the arches of the portico, glancing in our direction and whispering to each other.

"Giovannino," Margherita groaned, "they've recognized you!"

"It's not the first time," I replied calmly, "that I've gone somewhere and people have recognized me."

"But it may be the last! Just look, Giovannino, at their expressions!"

The expressions were not, to tell the truth, remarkably cordial. They were, to be somewhat more precise, rather sullen.

"My God!" cried Margherita. "The child!"

The Pasionaria had come out of the portico with an enormous ice-cream cone in her hand. One of the men called her over as she passed, and pointing to us, asked her a question.

The Pasionaria nodded.

"Now look!" cried Margherita. "They've asked her if you're you and she's told them you are."

The one who had asked if I was I stood talking to the Pasionaria. The Pasionaria replied with a shrug of her shoulders. Then she drew away and, still licking that tremendous ice-cream cone, disappeared under the portico.

"She's clever!" cried Margherita. "She's managed to get away. Let's hope she's smart enough to go to the police. . . . Look!"

The group had now increased somewhat, and the dark looks were still turned in our direction, and the gestures did indeed seem rather menacing.

Then one of the men leapt onto a bicycle and pedaled rapidly away.

"I'm sure of it, Giovannino!" cried Margherita. "He's gone to get the rest of the gang."

"Don't be so silly, Margherita. There are about fifteen of them already, and that's plenty if they had violence in mind."

Out of a street at the other end of the square came some men on bicycles, headed by an enormous man with a surly face, and the boy who had bicycled off before.

"Didn't I tell you, Giovannino? There's the gang!"

The huge man and his companions leaned their bicycles against the columns and joined the group under the portico.

"The big man," said Margherita, "is the leader of the gang."

Apparently this time she was right: they were all telling him something, and he was listening attentively, glancing every now and then toward us and nodding his head.

One of the gang had told the big man to look to the left, and there was the Pasionaria, who, having devoured the cone, was now headed directly toward the gang.

The big man stood in front of her and put one of his enormous hands on her shoulder. Then he leaned over and asked her something.

The Pasionaria looked up at him and nodded.

He took his hand off her shoulder, spoke for a moment to the thin boy who had called him, then leaned down to talk to the Pasionaria again.

The boy, meanwhile, had gone to get his bicycle. The big man now put his hands on the Pasionaria's waist, lifted her up, and sat her on the bar of the boy's bicycle.

It all happened so quickly that by the time it was done it was too late. The boy was already pedaling off into the unknown with his prey.

Margherita grabbed my arm.

"Don't move, Giovannino!" she cried. "They're not going to do anything to her, I can feel it. They only want to get rid of a dangerous witness—an innocent eye!"

The big man muttered something to several members of the gang, then slowly rolled up his shirt sleeves, pulled the brim of his hat down over his forehead, and began a slow march in our direction.

"Quick, Giovannino!" sobbed Margherita. "Start the car! Let's get out! You can't fight them all!"

The big man was now only a few inches from the car. He looked at me sullenly for a moment, then jerked his hat away and leaned his head in through the open window of the car. Our faces were now but a palm's breadth apart.

He hesitated for a moment or two, then in a deep voice said: "Diesel?"

"Yes," I replied. "Mercedes-Benz."

"Overhead cam?"

"Yes," I replied.

The man straightened and looked at the car. Then he leaned in again.

"Can I lift the hood?" he asked.

"Certainly," I replied.

He lifted the hood, the whole gang gathered around, and there ensued an animated discussion about the motor.

The discussion went on for quite some time. Then they all gathered around my window, and the big man took the initiative again.

"What do you get out of it?"

"Sixteen kilometers to a liter."

"Cylinder displacement?"

"Thousand-nine."

"Pickup?"

"Good."

"Third?"

"Slow."

"Speed?"

"Hundred and ten."

"Injectors?"

"Excellent."

The fat man turned back to the gang, and they had a whispered conference. Then he turned to me again:

"Much noise?"

"Only in low."

Having made sure the gear was in neutral, I turned on the motor. The gang went back to the raised hood and stood looking at the motor. Then the leader of the gang moved to the back of the car and put his huge paw over the exhaust, to see whether or not the motor had a heart murmur. He rejoined his gang and they continued to study the motor for some time. Then he lowered the hood.

I turned off the motor. The big man came along beside my open window. He leaned in, his face surlier than ever. "All right, Signor Guareschi," he grumbled, putting a finger to his hat.

He left, along with his chief of state and the rest of the gang. They got on their bicycles and departed. The square, once again, was empty and silent.

Margherita sighed with exhaustion. "The baby. . . ."

The baby was sitting peacefully on the handlebars, demolishing an ice cream cone even larger than the one she had had earlier. A few feet away the boy braked, lowered the Pasionaria to the ground, and left.

All was in order.

"I wanted lemon, and they didn't have any here," said the Pasionaria quietly as she rejoined us. "So that monkey gave me a ride to the next town."

"You might have thanked him," said Margherita in a low, terribly distant voice.

"Why?" asked the Pasionaria. "I paid him. A fifty-lire ice cream."

Margherita, still hardly audible, asked me for a cigarette. I lit it for her. She took several deep drags, then suddenly pressed my arm as though gripped by fear. Standing by her window was a huge priest, all in black, with a sullen face.

He leaned in. "Respectable women don't smoke in public," he said. His voice sounded deep and threatening.

"She's not respectable," replied the Pasionaria cheerfully. The priest, having identified the origin of the voice, drew back in horror, turned his great shoulders, and with a shake of his head started off.

Then he paused. He came back, walked around the car, leaned in my window.

"Diesel?" he asked brusquely.

"Diesel."

"Overhead cam?"

"Overhead cam."

He raised the hood and studied the motor attentively from both sides, then looked up at me and wiggled the first finger of his right hand. I turned the motor on. He gave it his attention for quite some time, then went around to the back to feel the exhaust.

He came to the front again and held up the palm of a hand as large as a hoe. I turned off the motor. He lowered the hood. He pressed down on a mud guard to test the suspension. He kicked one of the tires.

He put a finger to his hat, turned, and made off. After a few feet, he stopped and turned back.

"The King!" he shouted. "What's a King?" His face was grim. "The only King that matters is that one!"

He jerked his head in the direction of the church. The door was ajar. One could see candles flickering at the high altar.

He marched resolutely off toward the door of the rectory.

The square was silent and empty.

Soon our friend Mario reappeared with Albertino.

"Have you been bored?" Mario asked, as he climbed into the car.

"Not me," said the Pasionaria.

The car rumbled on, and soon we were on the white

road that crossed the great embankment. At the far end were the poplars and the river and—under the wide blue sky—all my stories.

"Diesel?" whispered Margherita.

"Diesel."

THE EXCUSE

We reached home late from the city, and the minute we got into the kitchen, the Pasionaria asked: "What time is dinner?"

"In the country you don't eat dinner, you eat supper," replied Margherita, who was mashing potatoes.

"Supper or dinner," grumbled the Pasionaria, "the important thing is to get it over with. I have a lot of homework to do."

Margherita paid no attention to her, and went on mashing potatoes.

The Pasionaria inspected the pots on the stove.

"Pasta with ragout, sausages and mashed potatoes!" she cried. "Well, that means I eat an egg."

"We're getting harder to please every day," Margherita

remarked. "Now we turn our nose up at pasta and sausage."

"They're all right," said the Pasionaria. "But when a person has work to do, she can't eat heavy stuff like that. Don't worry about it, I'll make my own."

She put a pan on the stove, then asked where the eggs were.

"I've got to eat right away," she said, "so I'll have time for my homework."

She had an egg fried in butter, a cup of broth, and a bit of cheese. She ate in silence.

After she had finished, the pasta arrived on the table.

"You can put a plate of it aside," said the Pasionaria to Margherita. "I'll eat it after I've finished my work. When you've been traveling around the way we have, cold stuff's all right too."

"Better eat it now," Albertino advised her, "while it's hot."

"You don't think it will interfere with my work?" asked the Pasionaria.

Albertino didn't think so, and the Pasionaria ate a good-sized plate of pasta.

Then the sausage with mashed potatoes came to the table; the Pasionaria eyed the platter sadly.

"If I didn't have work to do, I'd eat some," she murmured. "But if you've got to work, you can't eat sausage."

The cat came to claim what was rightfully his, and the sausage casing was passed to him.

The Pasionaria watched him eating, then shook her head sadly.

"Lucky cat!" she cried. "No worries, no homework!"

To see a child envying a cat was too much for me. I

handed the Pasionaria a generous helping of sausage and mashed potatoes.

After she'd eaten the lot, she cried out bitterly: "I knew it! Now my stomach feels as though I'd eaten cement."

Stewed fruit, well-sugared and eaten warm, is an aid to digestion; I set her down a plate of it. Then I thought she'd clear off.

"I'd rather do my work here," she said. "If I work alone at night in my room, I get depressed."

After the table was cleared, the Pasionaria took books and notebooks out of her school bag and set to work. But before she was able to get a word down, the point of her pen broke. She put in another point, which dropped a large glob of ink on the page. Her eraser now demonstrated that it was an even more imperfect working tool: instead of eradicating the glob, it spread it and then tore the paper. But the Pasionaria remained undaunted. She got rid of the torn page, only to find fresh trouble in the pen point: it now had a hair on it. The Pasionaria tried to remove it, but her efforts were vain, for this was the most obstinate pen point in the universe. Having no others, she took up a pencil, but the point broke.

Margherita, who had been silent till then, cried: "That's enough!"

She gathered the books and the notebooks from the table, threw them somewhat violently into the school bag, put the bag away, and set in front of me a fountain pen and a pad of paper with some envelopes.

"Try not to be too witty," she admonished me. "This isn't your newspaper nonsense, this has to be something serious and thoughtful—she's an old-fashioned school-teacher."

I quickly wrote off a few lines, then began to read aloud: " 'Dear madam, Today our Carlotta—' "

"For heaven's sake!" cried Margherita. "*Our* Carlotta! As though you were saying our President, or something!"

I changed it: " 'Today my Carlotta—' "

"Too intimate," Margherita decided. "Don't forget you're talking to a schoolteacher, an official, not one of your old cronies."

" 'Today Carlottina—' "

"Even worse!" cried Margherita. "Carlottina combines the defects of both 'our Carlotta' and 'my Carlotta.' "

" 'Today little Carlotta—' "

"Affected! If you want to apply an attribute to your daughter, choose one recognized as valid by the school authorities, not one arising out of paternal affection or literary caprice!"

" 'Today the child Carlotta—' "

"Vague! Evasive!"

" 'Today the daughter of the undersigned—' "

Margherita began to laugh.

" 'The daughter of the undersigned!' If you start off that way, you'll have to say things like, 'The undersigned humbly petitions,' and so on. In addition, it's absurd because 'the daughter of the undersigned' sounds like 'the daughter of the regiment' and things like that."

I was getting annoyed.

" 'Little Carlotta' is no good; 'the child Carlotta' is no good. So what do you want me to write? 'Citizen Carlotta'?"

The Pasionaria joined in.

"You could put 'Miss Carlotta,' " she said.

"Fancy that!" cried Margherita. "Calling a child 'Miss'!"

" 'Today the student Carlotta Guareschi—' "

"You'd think a man who makes his living writing could do better than that. However, it's all right. Go on."

" 'Today the student Carlotta Guareschi had to go off to the city—' "

"How amazing! A child so independent she goes off to the city on her own!"

" '—had to go off to the city with me.' "

"If the student Carlotta goes to the city in the third person, then she goes with her father and not with a fellow in the first person."

" 'Today the student Carlotta Guareschi had to go off to the city with her father, and as she returned late, was unable to complete her homework. Consequently, I hope you will excuse—' "

"How do *you* get into it?" Margherita interrupted excitedly. "If the student Carlotta Guareschi goes to the city with her father, then her father's the one who has to ask the teacher to excuse her. Not *you!*"

"But I'm her father."

"In the first person, yes. However, your daughter went to the city with her father in the third person. It's a question of two different authorities."

I found a brilliant solution.

" 'Today the student Carlotta Guareschi had to go off to the city with her father, and as I brought her home late, she was unable to complete her homework. Consequently, I hope—' "

"That isn't right!" cried Margherita. "The student Carlotta goes to the city with her father and comes home with you. Why didn't she come home with her father?"

"These matters don't concern the schoolteacher," I replied. "The student Carlotta goes with whomever she likes and comes back with whomever she likes."

"A fine picture you're giving of your daughter's respectability!"

"I don't get it," said the Pasionaria. "When the teacher sees Papa's signature, she'll know he has the same name as me, so even if the student Carlotta doesn't come home from the city with her father, the teacher won't be surprised because she'll realize it isn't just anybody but an uncle or anyway somebody in the family."

"Also," added Albertino, "when the student Carlotta came home, I was in the car too, and I can be a witness."

Margherita said in that case I could go on.

I went on.

"'. . . Consequently, I hope you will excuse her.'"

"Consequently's no good," said Margherita. "It's a literary adverb that would go all right in the city, but here we are out in the country."

"Consequently," I remarked, "is not an adverb."

"A pronoun, then."

"No, it's not that either."

"The very fact that I don't know what it is is proof enough that it's not in general use. It's precious and literary."

"'Therefore I hope—'"

"'Therefore' is too assertive. Too emphatic. It weakens the concept. Say 'hence.' If you say 'hence,' you give the teacher full liberty to believe or not to believe the excuse, relying on her personal kindness."

I relied on the teacher's personal kindness and changed 'therefore' to 'hence.'

I wrote out a good copy, put the letter in an envelope, and handed it to the Pasionaria.

"Well, it's all right this time," mumbled the Pasionaria. "But I warn you, from now on if you want me to go with you you'll have to write the excuse ahead of time."

I went to bed with a headache. Half an hour later Margherita joined me, remarking reprovingly: "A fine way to bring up children! You take the girl to the city and then let her come home with the first person she runs into."

I didn't answer; the father of the student Carlotta advised me to let the subject drop.

THE GENERATION
OF MUZIO SCEVOLA

Margherita was sitting, dispirited, in an armchair, suffering in silence.

"What's the matter, Margherita?" I asked.

Her eyes were sad as she looked up at me.

"Don't worry." She sighed. "Just leave me alone with my pain."

"Is this pain of yours," I asked, "localized, or is it diffused?"

"Diffused," replied Margherita, "in a localized body." Her voice was anguished. "Or rather, localized in a diffused body."

"Keep your paradoxes, Margherita," I said, "for some other occasion."

Her smile was melancholy.

"But it's not a paradox, Giovannino," she rejoined. "My suffering has reached the point where I feel that the pain has disintegrated all of me and scattered the pieces to the four winds. I'm not localized any more, I'm diffused."

This was the first time Margherita had felt diffused, and it bothered me.

"In order to reintegrate yourself, Margherita," I said, "you'll have to find out what caused the disintegration. Your suffering arises from some physical pain which has to be localized in the material portion of your being—and that, after all, is still intact."

"Nothing about me is still intact!" cried Margherita hopelessly. "My spiritual unity has been destroyed, my physical unity is mere nonsense. I'm like an apple which has no more meat, only an empty skin. I'm the husk of myself!"

"But, Margherita, the husk of yourself has physical consistency, which you must take into account if you are to reintegrate your being. We must try to discover which portions of the husk are unhealthy."

She shook her head. "If someone is dead, why try to cure the shadow?"

"But it's not a shadow I want to cure, Margherita, it's a body! A body which, at this particular moment, is sitting in that armchair and possesses total physical unity."

"It also," added the Pasionaria, "possesses a toothache."

Margherita looked at her scornfully. "Have some respect," she cried, "for your mother's remains!"

"You've got a toothache," repeated the Pasionaria.

"She hasn't," protested Albertino, who, quite clearly, was more inclined to the romantic idea of spiritual dispersion.

"She has," cried the Pasionaria. "I know it's true because she keeps touching her cheek and every once in a while she sucks in air."

Albertino looked at Margherita suspiciously.

"Is that true, Mama?" he asked.

"Pay no attention to her," said Margherita. "She's a slanderer."

"Very well," the Pasionaria cried, "if I'm a slanderer, let's see you drink cold water!"

She looked at Albertino, who went out to the kitchen and was soon back with a glassful of ice water.

"Drink it, Margherita," I said, holding the glass to the lips of the diffused woman.

Margherita looked up at me. "So you don't trust me!" she cried bitterly.

"Drink it," I repeated.

Margherita took one sip of water, then pushed the glass away and brought a trembling hand to her cheek.

A gleam of triumph shone in the Pasionaria's eyes.

Albertino went to Margherita's side. "Come on," he said. "The car's still out. Put on your coat and Papa will take you to the dentist."

"Not now," said Margherita. "Tomorrow."

"No," Albertino declared. "You must go right away."

"When we have a toothache," added the Pasionaria,

"you make us go to the dentist right away. Now you have to go right away too."

Margherita sat there trembling.

"It's nothing any more," Albertino assured her. "They have things to make the tooth go to sleep and you don't feel anything."

Margherita's trembling increased.

"So much fuss about going to the dentist!" cried the Pasionaria. "I've been thirty thousand times and I've never even said ouch."

"How can you possibly understand?" Margherita groaned. "You belong to another generation! Everything was already there for you—penicillin, painless dentists, telephones, elevators, cars, radios, vacuum cleaners, re-frigerators—"

"What's refrigerators got to do with it?" asked the Pasionaria.

"All these things seem natural to you!" Margherita shouted. "But we belong to a different generation, to a time when everything was difficult and painful. Just as we're still afraid to enter an elevator because elevators are a novelty for us, something very strange, so we're afraid to go to the dentist because when we were young the den-tist's office was like a torture chamber. . . ."

"Well, you're not young any more," said the Pasionaria firmly. "You're old, and you've got a toothache, so you have to go to the dentist right away and he won't hurt you."

"He *will* hurt me!" Margherita shrieked.

"He won't," declared Albertino, who had already brought Margherita her coat. "Come on, it'll all be over in an hour."

Margherita was still trembling.

"An old lady," said the Pasionaria with a loud laugh, "who's afraid to go to the dentist!"

"I'm not old and I'm not afraid," Margherita protested indignantly. "It's only that I've got the complex of the older generation. Your children will laugh at you when you're afraid to go to the moon on a space ship."

"But meanwhile," shouted the Pasionaria, "we're doing the laughing!"

I decided I had better break it up.

"Margherita," I said softly, "this older-generation thing is true. But don't forget your children belong to the younger generation, and it's their parents' duty to set an example for them—even if it means a terrible sacrifice."

Margherita rose.

"Very well," she said proudly, "I'll go to the dentist now. And I'll go with a smile on my face."

There was indeed a smile on her face as she put on her coat and headed for the door.

When we were in the car, she turned to the troupe that had come to witness the departure.

"And I am not," she declared, "going to a painless dentist, I'm going to an old-fashioned one, the kind that made us suffer so terribly when we were children. If I tried to avoid the pain, I would feel I was betraying my own youth. Our generation may regard the elevator and the airplane with suspicion—but we're not afraid of pain!"

At the pride in her words, Albertino and the Pasionaria both turned pale and found themselves unable to reply.

"Farewell!" called Margherita sarcastically, "farewell to the generation of the anesthesia! The generation of Muzio Scevola salutes you!"

"The generation of Muzio Scevola?" I asked as I put the car in gear. "Aren't you aging rather quickly, Margherita?"

"I say generation of Muzio Scevola to mean men who were able to look dry-eyed at the scalpel that was about to carve their living flesh—men who had so much self-respect they refused to give up anything that was properly theirs, even the pain of their flesh under the surgeon's knife!"

We were soon in the city. The generation of Muzio Scevola left the car in a parking lot, went to a drug store to buy a complete assortment of toothache remedies, and then continued on to the movies.

We got back late.

"All done?" the Pasionaria and Albertino asked me, after Margherita had gone up to her room.

"All done," I replied. "It was a very long painful business. He had to cut the gum and grind the bone."

"How did she behave?" asked Albertino.

"Magnificently! Not a cry out of her. And she refused the anesthesia."

The Pasionaria looked perplexed. "What's anesthesia?"

"The stuff that keeps you from feeling pain when you have an operation."

They were both much impressed.

"Were you there when they did it all?"

"Of course."

"Didn't it make you sick?"

Before going to the movies, I had bought two bags of roasted chestnuts and had eaten the lot; and just at that moment I felt as though there was a wild beast in my stomach; yet somehow I found the strength to laugh.

That night the generation of Muzio Scevola had no dinner: the masculine half, because it had a shocking stomach ache; the feminine half, because it had a horrible toothache. There was the compensation, however, of being able to look down, with foodless pride, at the total moral defeat of the generation of the anesthesia.

PURGATORY CAKE

It was the day before the Pasionaria's ninth birthday, and she wanted assurance that we were aware of it.

"Of course," said Margherita. "Everything's under control."

"How about the cake with the nine candles?" asked the Pasionaria. "I don't want to feel ashamed in front of my friends."

"It'll be all right," I said. "I'll buy it in town tomorrow morning."

"Not at all," said Margherita. "I'm going to make the cake myself."

This was serious. The Pasionaria and Albertino looked at me in horror.

"Margherita," I murmured, "why wear yourself out? You've already done too much."

Margherita shook her head. "A mother's first duty is to

bake her children's birthday cakes with her own hands."

The tone of Margherita's voice was final, and the Pasionaria and Albertino turned pale.

"But if you do too much," observed the Pasionaria, "then you'll say you have a headache and I'll feel guilty—"

"I won't say a word. Mothers have to suffer in silence. As soon as we've had our coffee, you two will go to bed, and I'll bake the cake."

"Do you know how to make Paradise cake?" asked Albertino.

"No," replied Margherita.

"What she'll make is Purgatory cake," grumbled the Pasionaria, as she rose from the table.

"Will you be quiet!" Margherita cried.

"That's the way it always is," said the Pasionaria. "When my birthday comes, everybody takes advantage of it. If it was his birthday, you'd have bought the cake."

"And for yours I'm going to make it! You ought to be ashamed, saying things like that when my every thought is to make you happy!"

"I don't eat thoughts," said the Pasionaria. "I eat cake." She left the kitchen.

Albertino followed without a word, but the look he gave me was a desperate one.

Margherita finished her cigarette, then rose.

"I've got a very good recipe," she said. "The cake's as light as a feather, and it doesn't have any of those awful fats that make most cakes so indigestible. It's just eggs, sugar, corn starch, and a little baking powder."

As a matter of fact, what Margherita should have done, to make her cake even more digestible, was leave out the eggs, sugar, corn starch, and baking powder as well.

However, I could hardly tell her that, so I asked her what I could do to help.

"You get the stove good and hot, that's all. But first I wish you'd weigh out the sugar and the corn starch—here's the recipe."

I did all this very carefully, then put some wood in the stove, and stood around watching.

Margherita worked with great authority and skill: anybody who had never tried one of her cakes would have said, "There's a woman born to bake cakes!"

Now is the moment to explain that Margherita's cakes aren't bad, they're just terrible. Indeed, Margherita bakes cakes as she reasons. Using a rigid logic all her own, Margherita reaches conclusions that are the most logically illogical in the world.

Eggs, corn starch, sugar. Margherita accepts this basis, and begins beating the eggs and the sugar together in a bowl. Then she decides the mixture is too thick, and she adds a bit of Marsala. Having, in this way, obtained a mixture that is too thin, she adds some graham crackers; then she forces the whole mixture through the meat grinder; and so on and so on.

Margherita worked with great authority for some three quarters of an hour, at the end of which time she handed me a baking pan filled to the brim with a delicately yellow mixture.

"Just put this in the oven," she said. "Every once in a while, stick a toothpick in it, and when the toothpick comes out dry, take the cake out of the oven and let it cool. Then you can decorate it with this whipped cream and a little imagination, arrange the nine candles, and put it in the pantry."

She went peacefully off to bed, and I sat down in front of the oven, to stand guard over the cake. Every once in a while I opened the oven door to see what was going on.

At first the cake made no move at all save to turn a rather golden brown. Then, as the baking powder went into action, it began to swell, until finally it touched the top of the oven. Slowly it began to go back to normal, and after a time was no higher than the pan, but it must have had trouble with the brakes, for it kept getting lower and lower.

I decided to try a toothpick, but the toothpick wouldn't go through the top of the cake. It simply broke. I managed to get a nail through, however, and when the nail came out wet, I closed the oven door. At that moment the kitchen door opened, and in came Albertino and the Pasionaria in their pajamas.

"How's it going?" asked the Pasionaria.

"It's baking."

"How does it look?" asked Albertino.

"Hard to say, it's not ready yet."

We waited about ten minutes more and then had a look. The cake had fallen even lower. We managed to get a nail into it, and the nail came out dry.

I took the cake out of the oven and put it on the table.

"It looks like a pancake," Albertino remarked rather cautiously.

Now the Pasionaria tried to put the nail into it, but didn't even succeed in scratching the top.

"We'll need a drill," she said, "to get the candles in."

"Or we could attach them," said Albertino, "with carpenter's glue."

"That won't be necessary," I said. "Once we put the

whipped cream on it, it'll look all right and the candles will stand in the cream."

We put the cake into the refrigerator. It cooled very quickly. Then we turned the pan upside down on the kitchen table, and as the cake fell out, it sounded like a piece of wood.

It was somewhat less than an inch high, and when you struck it, it returned slowly to normal, for it had maintained a fair degree of elasticity.

We stood looking for a time in silence at the cake that should have been the lightest and most digestible in the world.

The Pasionaria's sigh was hardly audible.

"Poor Mama," she said. There were tears in her eyes.

"There's no need to dramatize the thing," I said. "We're going to counterattack. And don't forget, you're not fighting for a cake, children, you're fighting for your mother!"

I put the cake back into the oven. When I took it out again, it was as thin as a biscuit.

The problem was how to soften it. I broke off a piece and tried dipping it in milk, but it absolutely refused to absorb a drop. We then hammered it into small pieces and put it through the meat grinder.

I put the powder thus obtained into a bowl and added some Moscato wine: the result was a sluggish mass that boded no good.

I added flour, eggs, and sugar, but the mixture seemed very hard and lumpy, no doubt because the meat grinder was not as efficient as it ought to have been.

"We could make a kind of pastry," said the Pasionaria, "and then press it out with the iron."

This suggestion gave me a brilliant idea. I broke the mixture into small pieces and put them through the rollers of the machine that makes pasta. When I put all the sheets together, they formed a fairly compact mass.

"If we cook it that way," said the Pasionaria, "it'll come out like a brick."

"And," added Albertino, "it'll never rise."

"True," I said. "It's been devitalized by the rude treatment it's received. We'll have to liven it up."

We dried it out in the oven, grated it, added milk and Marsala, then some baking powder, and mixed the whole thing together: the result was soft and smooth.

We buttered a pan, poured the mixture in, and put the pan in the oven.

It was clear to us, after a few minutes, that the mixture was somewhat too lively, so we took the pan out of the oven again and put a heavy lid over it, which we wired down, so that the mixture would be confined and forced to restrain its ebullience.

We put it back into the oven. We were then faced with the problem of how we were to tell when it was finished. To take the lid off would have been like breaking one of the master dams of the Po in full spate.

The Pasionaria got the drill, and we punctured holes in the lid at five or six points. From time to time we put toothpicks through the holes.

When the cake was finished, we took the pan out of the oven and let it cool. Then we freed it from the cover and trimmed it with scissors, where the lid and the top of the pan didn't exactly meet.

"To do a really good job," the Pasionaria remarked, "we should have soldered them together."

Although the cake seemed to be cooked, it did not present a very attractive appearance, because in many places the top of it had stuck to the covering.

"Now we really do need the iron," said the Pasionaria, who was a farsighted woman.

I had one slight improvement, however. I sprinkled powdered chestnut over the top, filling in all the holes, and then very carefully ran a hot iron over it. The top now looked firm and bright; we put powdered sugar over it.

The cake did not seem to be quite so light as might be desired, so Albertino went to my workroom and got my spray gun, and I inundated the cake with a light shower of white wine.

We then went on to the decoration: whipped cream, nuts, bits of candy, raisins, and crystallized fruit. After we added the nine candles, we admired the masterpiece briefly, then put it into the refrigerator.

It was dawn; we were exhausted; but Margherita was safe.

The cake looked splendid when it came to the table after dinner.

But after each of us had a slice on our plates, we looked at one another in perplexity: who was going to be the first to try it?

The Pasionaria, strong and generous as always, made the supreme sacrifice and swallowed a large mouthful.

"Extraordinary!" she cried.

It was, in truth, a very good cake; and Margherita was loaded with praise.

"It's all in a day's work," she said coolly. "I can do a lot better."

HAMLET

I met Hamlet at Hamlet's and Hamlet made me a present of him.

Although this may sound complicated, it's actually quite simple: Hamlet is the dog that was given to me by Hamlet who is the proprietor of the restaurant called Hamlet's.

In strictest truth, Hamlet, when Hamlet gave him to me, wasn't called Hamlet. He had no name or shape—he was just a bundle of soft black stuff with a very imprecise outline.

"What is he?" I asked Hamlet.

"He must be a dog," Hamlet replied.

"What breed?"

"Hard to say. He's like his mother, he's a lot of breeds."

I lifted the black bundle up from the ground to have a better look, and he licked my nose. He did it gracefully and with a sense of restraint which I found attractive.

I put him down again and Hamlet hoisted him up onto the step. The dog then decided to abandon the little outdoor tables I was sitting at, and go inside the restaurant.

"What's his name?" I asked Hamlet.

"He didn't have any identification papers when he arrived. We don't know anything about him."

After I'd begun to eat, I decided I wanted a vegetable, so I called out for Hamlet. The puppy appeared on the step instead, looked up at me, and gave out a kind of creaking sound.

When he saw that I was paying no attention to him, he went back inside, and I called again for Hamlet. And once again the black bundle appeared, looked up at me, and creaked.

In a moment Hamlet appeared as well, and after I'd discussed the subject of vegetables with him, I said: "I know the puppy's name."

Then I turned toward the window of the restaurant and called: "Hamlet!"

The black bundle appeared in the doorway, looked up at me, and tried again to bark.

"This," I said to Hamlet, "is the third time that phenomenon has been observed. Clearly the dog's name is Hamlet."

"Professor," Hamlet muttered, in a less than friendly voice, "you're a great one for jokes."

"I'm not joking," I replied, "any more than I'm a professor. And if you don't like me to say the dog's name is Hamlet, I won't say it any more. The dog's name is not Hamlet. Okay? But he's a dog that answers to the name of Hamlet."

The bundle had gone back into the restaurant. I shouted, "Hamlet!" and he came back at once, and again gave his puppyish imitation of a bark.

But Hamlet was still not convinced. As the black bundle had disappeared again, we now tried calling him by other names: Alcibiades, Flick, Bob, Themistocles,

Othello, and so on. None brought him forth. The minute I called, "Hamlet!" again, however, there he was in the doorway.

Things being thus, I considered it permissible to state the case more clearly.

"The dog's name," I said, "is not Hamlet, but he evinces a lively desire to be called Hamlet. What do we do? Do we satisfy his desire?"

"There can't be more than one Hamlet at Hamlet's," said Hamlet. "I'm not going to compete with a dog."

I could understand that Hamlet had no desire for a competition of this nature. On the other hand, if the dog wanted to be called Hamlet, was it fair to ignore the fact entirely? One should aid the young in their desire to find a name, not impede them.

I found a compromise solution.

"We'll call him Hamlet," I said to Hamlet, "and he can come and live in the country with me."

"All right," Hamlet replied. "Call him Hamlet then!"

He had spoken the last words rather loudly, and the black bundle had, almost at once, appeared in the doorway. Hamlet picked him up by the scruff of the neck, opened the door of my car, which was parked in front of the restaurant, and chucked him onto the back seat.

"Have a good trip," he muttered as he closed the door.

The puppy now began to whimper, at which his mother came to the doorway and stood looking, with a worried air, first at the car and then at Hamlet.

"Forget about him, Kitty," said Hamlet. "He's gone over to the far right, along with the other farmers."

The bitch expressed her pleasure at the new political

line her son had adopted by trotting off with her tail wagging happily.

Hamlet behaved rather badly that night—he declared at length and loudly that he did not intend to be left alone—and then at last he fell silent. But when I came out of my bedroom in the morning, I found an object in the doorway that should not have been there.

It shouldn't have been there if only because, as Hamlet wasn't able to climb the one step from the sidewalk to the floor of his maternal restaurant without help, I couldn't understand how he'd managed to climb two entire flights of steps during the night and get down again.

Then too, once he'd left his lively message of protest at my door, why didn't he stay up there?

I decided, in any case, that Hamlet needed a severe reprimand. When I got downstairs, I found him lying in the place I'd assigned to him, at the foot of the steps, pretending to be asleep. I picked him up by the scruff of the neck and held him right in front of me, so that he would realize, when he saw the lightning that flashed from my eyes, how serious was the sin that he had committed.

He licked me apprehensively on the nose.

I forgave his ill-advised nocturnal action and turned him loose in the garden, suggesting that he guard it well while I prepared for the trip to the country, and asking him to pay special attention to the car.

When I went out again, Hamlet came running toward me to tell me the news: he had turned pale blue.

I touched him. There was no question about it—it was

motor oil. I had lubricated the car the evening before, and Hamlet had checked the job thoroughly.

I gave him a careful cleaning with gasoline, but after a couple of minutes he began to tumble about excitedly, trying to scratch himself everywhere at once. So, to eliminate the cause of the irritation, I massaged him well with talcum powder. To get rid of the powder, I went over him with the vacuum cleaner.

Hamlet gave evidence of a sterling character, for he neither squirmed nor opened his mouth during this long operation. When it was finished, he licked my nose. The licking smelled strongly of motor oil.

"Hamlet," I said to him, "no doubt mechanical progress fascinates you as it fascinates all simple souls, but don't allow yourself to be seduced by it, don't mistake it for civilization. Even though men may be unworthy of their manhood, you must not betray your doghood."

On our way out to the country, Hamlet behaved extremely well. He never barked except when I blew the horn—not an excessive reaction on the part of a dog traveling in a car for the first time.

When after a time I blew the horn and Hamlet barked but without the sound accompaniment, I realized he must have a dry throat. We stopped at the next roadside café. As a matter of fact, it was hot, and I was thirsty too, so we sat down at a table and both of us wet our throats.

Then Hamlet expressed a desire to take a little walk, which I decided to permit, but this was the first time he had done any traveling and he was unfamiliar with the dangers of the road. I soon heard him calling desperately for me. I ran outside. A few feet away the road was being resurfaced, and Hamlet, having ignored all the warning signs, had gone dashing onto the freshly laid tar and was stuck there now like a fly.

The road workers were friendly people, and they gently released the bundle of soft fur from the black flypaper.

"My advice to you," said the man who handed Hamlet over to me, "is to send him to the dry cleaner."

"I'd have him clipped," said the owner of the café.

But that was no good. If you clip a bundle of silk, what's left?

Nor did I care to repeat the episode of the gasoline. So I cleaned him with warm olive oil and cotton. At Piacenza I bought a package of powder for a foam bath (It removes all impurities without irritating the skin and at the same time imparts a delightful massage, thanks to its millions of tiny bubbles), and when we got home, I gave him a complete renovation.

Once again Hamlet behaved like a real man and I bestowed unreserved praise on him.

Then I showed him around the house, which he seemed to like. At any rate, he wagged his tail.

That was when I realized that Hamlet had an unbalanced posterior section.

I must attempt to explain this. Why has nature given dogs a tail? So they can wag it. And dogs, obediently enough, wag their tails. All this is what we call "natural." But surely it isn't "natural" if the wagging of a tail unbalances the owner of the tail. If the owner of the tail is unbalanced, either wholly or in part, in the process of wagging the tail, that means there is some defect in the assembly—or else that the dog has been supplied with a tail of greater capacity than is suitable to his make.

When Hamlet, then, began to wag his tail, his anterior

section remained firmly attached to the ground, while his posterior section became so agitated by the lateral movement of the tail that it too began to slide from left to right.

"That dog has a tail beyond his strength," said a neighbor of mine who happened to be passing at the time and who had paused to observe the phenomenon. "It'll have to be cut."

"We have long been friends," I told him, "but if you ever dare to say anything so shocking again, we are friends no more."

"I didn't mean to offend you," he answered, "but almost all dogs have their tails cut—"

"Not Hamlet!" I cried. "Hamlet's not a dog, he's an idea in motion. Anyway, I'll find some way to anchor him down."

Hamlet asked permission to make a tour of the house, which I granted; a few minutes later, I heard him calling for me with desperation in his voice.

Synthetic enamels are, unquestionably, a devilish invention, and it was a synthetic enamel that a painter had just finished applying around the base of the garage. Executing an about-turn, Hamlet found that his tail had been attached horizontally to the enamel.

When he saw me, he began to wag his tail, but since it was immovable, he himself began to move, and so I was able to observe the impressive sight of a tail wagging a dog.

I got a chisel and knocked away the bit of plaster to which the tail was attached. This slight addition to the weight of the caudal mass unbalanced Hamlet's posterior section still further, as a result of which he was visibly embarrassed.

In an attempt to console him, I brought him into my study and showed him a large photograph of the family of which he was now a member.

"This is me," I told him, "and this is Margherita, this is Albertino, and this is the Pasionaria. They're nice people, all of them, and you're going to like them."

Diligently, Hamlet licked the entire family, and when I put him down seemed to be in a better frame of mind.

As he was about to leave, he noticed a piece of string on the floor. He clamped his teeth around it and began to worry it. Unfortunately, it wasn't a piece of string at all, it was the cord of my desk lamp, which, after Hamlet had gnawed through the wires, gave him a severe shock.

This time he complained a bit.

"Hamlet," I told him, "I've already warned you: put no trust in mechanical progress, seek to remain one with nature!"

A large bowl of milk helped to reaffirm his faith in life.

He agreed to sleep in the garage, but he wanted the light left on. I permitted it. Although I'm somewhat older than Hamlet, I too have a fear of the dark—more now, even, than when I was a child.

Hamlet, good night.

FIREWOOD

Here is an old story whose beginning is lost in the dark night of time—lost, more accurately, in a sultry July afternoon.

I had been driving for an hour over the bubbling asphalt of the Via Emiliana when I realized that the needle of the oil gauge had departed from its customary position toward the right and was now considerably left of center. I stopped the car, got out, lifted the hood, and checked the oil: it was, unquestionably, below minimum. But fortunately I had a reserve tin of it in the luggage compartment.

I went back and opened the door of the trunk, to find staring me in the face an enormous pile of firewood. Good, dry firewood, all cut and trimmed, just right for the stove. On a July afternoon, beneath a boiling sun, on the bubbling asphalt of the Via Emiliana.

How on earth had the wood ever got into the trunk of my car?

What lunatic at large had arranged it?

But this, obviously, was not the moment to attempt to solve the mystery. This was the moment to locate the tin of oil. Very cautiously I began to dismantle the wall of firewood, hoping to find, and remove, the tin of oil without first having to remove all the wood.

And, as things worked out, I didn't have to remove all the wood, because almost all the wood, after a moment or two, tumbled down onto my feet.

I took the tin, poured in the oil, and then had to consider what I was going to do about the wood. I couldn't just leave it there, on the side of the road. And wherever it came from, it was, after all, good honest firewood.

Besides, how can one pursue an inquiry without the *corpus delicti?*

I picked up the pieces of wood and threw them any old way into the trunk, after which I had to take them all out again and put them back carefully, one by one, to reconstruct the solid wall I had found. Even so, three logs were left over; these I gave lodging to inside the car.

When I got to Milan, there were so many annoying little things to be done that I completely forgot about the wood. I remembered it only three days later, on my way back. Halfway back, as a matter of fact, when I had to stop the car because at every lurch in the road something in the dim recesses of the car made the most infernal racket.

I opened the trunk to find that it was the oil tin that had been banging around.

It was then I remembered the wood.

But the wood had disappeared. There wasn't a suggestion of it, either in the trunk or inside the car.

The weather was terribly hot, I was tired and sleepy, and so I was willing to accept the first explanation that leapt into my mind: it had all been a dream, the memory of some silly dream that had got entangled in the memory of actual happenings. I forgot all about the wood.

One evening, some time later, not far from Milan, one of my tires began to go flat. I stopped and opened the trunk to get out the tool kit, but I didn't get very far: the trunk was full of wood. This time it wasn't a dream, it was real, brutally real, for the kit was under the firewood.

Profiting by experience, I took the wood out, this time piece by piece, and piled it, piece by piece, inside the car. I found the tools, changed the tire, and concluded my journey.

When I reached Milan, I put the car in the garage and went to bed. The next morning I went down to the garage to begin my investigation of the firewood mystery, only to find that the wood was no longer there.

I heard a peculiar noise coming from the cellar, I went quietly down the stairs—and there was Giuseppina, *in flagrante.*

She was piling up pieces of firewood!

"Where did you get that wood?" I asked.

She flushed and stammered out a few unintelligible noises.

Giuseppina, who comes in three days a week, is both reliable and taciturn: the kind of woman who has no idea how to tell a lie.

"Where did you get that wood?" I repeated sternly.

"I found it in your car," she replied.

"And who," I went on, "put it in my car?"

She made no reply. She shrugged and spread her arms.

My eyes, by now, were growing accustomed to the darkness of the cellar, and as I looked around, I made a most startling discovery. Giuseppina was piling the pieces of wood carefully, one on top of the other, but not against the wall! She was piling them against other pieces of wood—and what I had taken to be the wall of the cellar was in fact a wall of wood. It went all the way to the ceiling and was about six feet deep.

"And all that other wood there," I cried in my astonishment, "where did you get that?"

"It's always been in the trunk of your car. This is the first time it wasn't."

I said nothing more. Two days later I got back to base.

"Margherita," I said, "would you mind telling me the secret of the wood that travels around in my car?"

"Ah!" she replied. "So Giuseppina let you in on it!"

"No, Margherita, I let myself in on it. At least twice."

Margherita shrugged.

"It's not all that much of a secret," she said. "Next winter, when you're in Milan, instead of spending good money on bad wood, and wet in the bargain, you'll have good, dry wood that doesn't cost anything because it's yours—it comes from out here in the country, and if you didn't want to use it, why did you have so many trees cut down?"

"But didn't I tell you that when the time came I'd have a truckload sent to Milan?"

"Well, and didn't the wood get to Milan without a truck? The household economy, Giovannino, is my business, not yours."

A useless debate, obviously.

"Margherita," I cut it short, "the wood reached Milan secretly and illegally. All right, it's done now—but there mustn't be a next time, is that understood?"

Margherita nodded.

"Giovannino," she said, "your slightest wish is my command."

After my usual four days a week of country living, the time came for me to go back to Milan.

Before getting into the car, I looked into the trunk and found, as I had expected, that some criminal hand had filled it with wood.

I closed the trunk and called Margherita.

"Tell the garage to have a look at the filter, will you?" I said. "There's something wrong with the carburetor. I'll use the other car this morning."

I got in and left.

Margherita stood watching me, motionless as a statue. I had played my cards with devilish ingenuity; the last glance she gave me was full of contempt.

It was a lighthearted journey, and when I reached the outskirts of Milan and a couple of excise police stopped me to ask if I was carrying anything taxable, I laughed, got out of the car, and opened the trunk for them.

It was full of wood, full to the brim.

"That's a good one!" chortled one of the police. "An automobile that runs on wood!"

"I've never seen one of those," said the other. "Charcoal yes, but not wood."

They laughed at my astonishment.

"Didn't you know there's a tax on wood?" asked the first.

"No," I said.

"Then this is a very good time to learn."

"All right, tell me how much I've got to pay, and I'll pay it."

"It's not as easy as that," said the second. "You pay by weight. Anyway, let's stop kidding around. What have you got under the wood?"

I looked at him in astonishment.

"Under the wood?" I stammered. "What am I supposed to have under the wood?"

"Are you telling me, with a car like that, you travel around with a trunk full of firewood? You'll have to admit it's a bit peculiar."

I wanted to tell him that if he knew Margherita he'd find nothing peculiar in it at all. But I only said: "The wood's there for you to look at."

"Well, we'll look at it then. Park the car off the road over there and take all the wood out."

I parked the car where he told me and piece by piece removed the wood.

When the trunk was empty, the two policemen gave it a thorough going over, tapping the sides, examining the tool kit, opening the reserve can of oil, even checking on the spare tire.

"Now what?" I asked, after the examination was over.

"Now you put the wood back in the car and get out of here or I'll take you in for making a public nuisance of yourself. But first you give me your name and address— I've got to send in a report on this wood business."

In a way, I was lucky. There wasn't much traffic as yet on the highway, and so the number of passing motorists who gave me their moral support as I reloaded the wood was not great.

One and all, however, watched the spectacle with interest and amusement.

I spent my days in Milan feeling as though there was a live tiger in my gut and, when I got into the car to head back home, my designs were very close to criminal.

The journey began badly in the extreme: I had no

sooner reached the outskirts of Milan than I was stopped by the police again. After looking inside the car, they wanted to know what I had in the trunk. I got out and opened it for them.

"What's this stuff?" asked the officer in charge.

What answer could I make? The trunk *was* full of firewood.

"It's firewood," I said.

"Where are you coming from?"

"Milan."

"Where are you going?"

I told him I was going to join my family in the country.

"You buy your firewood in Milan? Isn't there any in the country where you live?"

"There's too much of it!" I cried. "But I didn't buy this wood, this wood is mine, from my own trees."

"Are you the owner of a forest in Milan?"

"The wood comes from trees on my farm in the country."

The officer looked at me with considerable surprise.

"If the wood comes from the country," he said, "how does it happen to be coming from Milan right now? Do you bring your wood to Milan for a visit?"

I got so confused, trying to answer, that the officer asked me to take the wood out so he could check the inside of the trunk.

I took the wood out and then I put it back again.

The officer told me he was sorry he'd made me waste so much time.

Here I did something rather brilliant. Instead of continuing on, I turned the car and headed back toward

Milan. The police watched me as though I had suddenly lost my mind.

Giuseppina was still home.

"Why didn't you take the wood out?" I asked.

"The wood? But your wife only told me to take the wood out of the other car, she never mentioned this one."

I told her to get the wood out at once, because I wasn't going to the country this week.

The next day, around eleven, Carletto drove up.

"You're still here?" he asked.

"Looks that way."

"It does, for a fact, but you left yesterday, and we had a date to meet out there this morning. I've just come from there. What happened?"

"Nothing much. Car trouble."

"Just as well. Okay if I leave my car here in your driveway?"

"Whatever you like."

Carletto opened the trunk of his car.

"Greetings from your wife," he said, as he left. "But get the stuff out, will you? I need the car."

I called Giuseppina and told her to unload the wood that had just arrived in Milan in the trunk of Carletto's car.

THE TOMATO COMPLEX

I heard the Pasionaria grumbling. She was angry at somebody or something, but that, of course, was her business.

Then she raised her voice.

"What I'd like to know," she said, "is why we buy mineral water in this house, and then somebody props his newspaper against it, and if you touch the bottle he begins to roar like a lion."

I took my newspaper away, so that the Pasionaria could have the bottle she was interested in.

"Anyway," said the Pasionaria, as she poured out some mineral water for herself, "you shouldn't read while you eat. It's bad for you. That's what Papa always says."

I didn't like the sarcastic tone in her voice and I turned to remark on it to Margherita. But Margherita wasn't there.

"Where is she?" I asked.

"Over there," said Albertino.

"Why isn't she eating?"

"She's got a new disease," said the Pasionaria.

I got up from the table and went over there, and found Margherita sitting in an armchair by the radio, staring fixedly at something in the opposite corner of the room, but when I looked, I couldn't see anything, so I asked Margherita what was wrong.

"I've got a complex," she said mournfully.

I told her I didn't understand.

"You'll understand," she said, with a sigh, "when I'm no longer here. You men always understand everything too late."

The conversation was taking a very bad turn; I tried to pin it down.

"Margherita, you tell me you've got a complex, but if you don't tell me exactly which complex you've got, how can I possibly understand? There are thousands of complexes! Which one have you got?"

"I don't know. I only know I've got a complex and I'm suffering terribly."

I sat down opposite her.

"Margherita," I said as gently as I could, "I know you pretty well, but if you don't tell me a little more exactly what's bothering you, how can we help you and heal you?"

"There's no need for me to be healed," said Margherita. "And if I die, what's the difference? Who am I? What do I mean? Who's even aware that I'm alive? Who would care if I were dead?"

I laughed shortly, and perhaps a bit cruelly.

Margherita's eyes filled with tears. "I want my children beside me!" she cried.

"No, Margherita," I said quietly, "I've already written the story of how you tell the children their poor mama is going to die and when she's buried she'll be so lonely and so on, I wrote that last year. Find something new, Margherita, if you really feel an irresistible desire to make your children cry. Let's go on talking about you, Margherita! What exactly is it that you feel?"

Margherita shook her head. "I don't know, Giovannino. Sometimes I feel something here—"

"Where's here?"

She smiled sadly. "No one has yet made a topographical map of suffering. How can you localize a pain that suddenly fills your entire soul?"

"Margherita, you don't have to endure a psychological disturbance in the same way you have to endure a brick that falls on your head. Let's try to analyze this pain of yours. If a sense of anguish suddenly invades your soul, at what point does the invasion begin?"

"The soul isn't a *thing!* It doesn't have a shape or a border, it has no center of gravity, it has no surface, no sides, no angles. So how can it have a *point?* Or do you imagine that instead of a soul I have a parallelepiped or a dodecahedron?"

I had never imagined anything of the sort, and I told her so. Then I tried to clarify my ideas for her.

"Margherita, listen to me for a minute. Does this feeling of anguish you have arise from inside you or from without?"

Margherita gave me a look of scorn.

"Do you think I carry my soul in my handbag?"

"Of course not, Margherita, I know very well your soul is within you. But very often psychological disturbances have a physical cause. If you put your mind to it, you may find that the anguish you feel *here* has its real origin in the heart, or the lungs, or the liver—and to cure the anguish, you need only cure the heart, or the lungs, or the liver. Or the spleen."

Margherita looked at me for quite a time in silence, her eyes narrowed.

"Giovannino," she said finally, "I find all this even more contemptible than historical materialism. It's geographical materialism. Actually, topographical materialism. I've had no particular scientific training, but I think I'm able to distinguish between a complex and a liver attack."

I asked her please not to get excited. We may now, I said, exclude the possibility that Margherita's anguish arose from some internal disfunction.

"In that case," I went on, "we must look for its origin in the outside world. Now, this psychological disturbance of yours, on constant repetition, becomes a chronic condition, but tell me one thing: are you sure that when you feel it, it's unexpected? That it has no immediate cause? Think back. Make sure that you don't feel this anguish of yours when one particular thing occurs. When, in other words, some external agent forces you to recall an unhappy experience, or, at any rate, some particular thing that you don't like."

Margherita looked discouraged.

"It's not all that difficult," I went on. "For example, a short man may dislike being short and so every time he sees a tall man, he feels a kind of annoyance that, on repetition, becomes chronic—becomes, in other words, a height complex. And that complex takes the form of hostility toward any object that may be called high, such as a skyscraper, or an obelisk, or things of that nature. The person who feels this hostility is, of course, unaware of it, for it's his subconscious that's at work. So the short man has no idea that he has a height complex. He feels the anguish but can't imagine why, for the anguish may be induced by external causes that have no specific factor but are merely further links in the chain. So try, Margherita, try to analyze your own feeling of anguish—we'll work our way back to the original cause, we'll isolate it, and we'll cure it. Now concentrate: this anguish that you're feeling now, how was it manifested? Where were you, what were you doing, what were you looking at when you felt the disturbance?"

Interested at last, Margherita began to concentrate. Then she called the children.

"You remember, a little while ago, I said, 'O God, it's here again! That thing's come back.' Where was I?"

Albertino and the Pasionaria had a private consultation, and when it was over had reached the decision that at the time Margherita said, "O God, it's here again! That thing's come back," she was standing in front of the kitchen cabinet.

"True!" Margherita cried. "I remember now. But does that mean I've got a kitchen cabinet complex?"

We went into the kitchen, and I told Margherita to stand in front of the cabinet.

"Was it open or closed?" I asked.

"Open," the Pasionaria declared.

I opened the cabinet door.

"Try to remember, Margherita," I said. "What were you doing?"

"I know what she was doing," said the Pasionaria. "She was pretending to put the pots and pans in order but actually she was eating spoonfuls of tomato paste—that stuff that comes in cans that you say not to eat as if it was marmalade because it's bad for you. She gets spots on her face and heartburn if she eats it, but she's the lady of the house, so she can eat as much as she wants."

"She's spying on me!" Margherita cried. "She's not a child, that one, she's the secret police!"

"When somebody does something underhanded," said the Pasionaria, undaunted, "that means the one who's wrong is the mother, not the daughter who happens to be watching her."

"That's enough of that!" I said. "Let's get on with our investigation. Now, Margherita, you were eating a spoonful of that tomato junk on the sly when suddenly you said, 'O God, it's here again! That thing's come back!' In one hand you had the can of tomato sauce, and in the other a spoon. It was either, then, your olfactory sense or your palate that was being affected—smell or taste."

"Now I remember!" cried Margherita. "It was the smell and taste of the tomato paste."

I expressed satisfaction.

"Now, Margherita, I want you to repeat exactly what you were doing when you felt the anguish."

Margherita leaned into the cabinet and swallowed two large spoonfuls of concentrated tomato paste.

"O God, it's here again!" she cried, after a moment. She turned. "That thing's come back! Giovannino, there's no doubt of it—I've got a tomato complex!"

This was too much for me.

"Margherita, when a short man sees a cavalry officer and feels a stab of pain, that doesn't mean he's got a cavalry-officer complex. It's the *height* of the cavalry officer that's causing the pain. Therefore we must try to find out what the taste or smell of tomato paste is linked to—the tomato paste itself may be only one link in a long chain. What is your immediate association with tomato paste?"

"Bicarbonate of soda," said the Pasionaria. "Every time she eats the sauce, she has to take bicarbonate."

This was a step forward.

"And what is associated with bicarbonate?"

"Salt!" cried Margherita. "Giovannino, I've got a salt complex! Once I made a mistake and put salt instead of bicarbonate into a glass, and now when I take bicarbonate I remember the disgusting taste of that salted water."

I filled a glass with water, put in a teaspoonful of salt, and stirred it.

"Drink this, Margherita, and tell me what your reaction is."

She drank it down; then, twisting her lips in disgust, she cried: "Sea water! Last year, when I was trying to learn to swim, I drank some. . . ."

We had found our way to the sea: it augured well.

"Quick now, Margherita, tell me—what is there about the sea that annoys you most?"

"The girls!" cried the Pasionaria. "When she's on the beach, she's always saying, 'How shameless they are, these girls today! When I was a girl. . . .' And so on. The usual dumb things old people say."

I spoke now with as much care and caution as I could muster.

"Margherita, I'm very sorry to have to say this to you, but what you have is an aged-forty complex."

"An aged-forty complex? Is that very serious, Giovannino?"

"I'm afraid so, Margherita. And you've had it for five years, if you think about it."

"Do you suppose not eating any more tomato paste will cure it?"

"No, Margherita. You need a more radical treatment. You must give up the forty-year-old point of view and move on to a—shall we say—higher bracket."

"Then I'll get an aged-fifty complex, won't I?"

"How can you, if you're only forty-five? You'll be five years ahead of the game."

Margherita paced excitedly up and down for a moment. Then she cried, with great decision: "You're only as old as you feel. And you're only as old as you look. I look about forty, don't I?"

I studied her very carefully.

"No," I said. "With the tip of your nose covered with tomato paste, as it is now, you look like a little girl."

At these words, Margherita turned pale. She sank into an armchair.

"O God!" she cried, "it's here again. That thing's back!"

The Pasionaria looked in at the door. She too had concentrated tomato paste on the tip of her nose.

But no complex.

THE SURVEY

A woman with a very gentle voice telephoned me to ask if I would grant her an extremely short interview for a woman's magazine. I told her at once that if she was going to try to get an opinion of women's fashions out of me, she'd got hold of the wrong man.

"It's nothing to do with fashion," she said. "It's a survey we're making. All you've got to do is answer this one question: 'Why did you marry your wife?' "

I wasn't too surprised: there had been so many surveys lately. "Which songs do you like best?" "If the Russians come, what will you do?" "If you were Truman, what would you have done?" And so on. I wasn't surprised, but I was puzzled.

"You'd like to know," I said, "why I married my wife?"

"That's it. Why did you marry your wife? It's a sensible question, I think. After all, a man marries one woman rather than another, so he must have a reason. Think about it for a second, then tell me."

I thought about it, but no answer came to me, so I told the woman at the other end of the telephone that it was a long time ago when I married my wife, and I no longer remembered why I'd married Margherita and not some other woman.

"Never mind," said the interviewer. "Take your time, think about it some more, I'll call you tomorrow."

I put the receiver down and went back into the breakfast room. Margherita looked at me suspiciously.

"What's going on?" she asked.

"They wanted to know why I married you."

"Is something wrong?" she asked, alarmed.

"No, Margherita, everything's fine. It's a magazine survey. I'm supposed to answer the question: 'Why did you marry your wife?' "

Margherita seemed relieved. She remarked that it would be better if journalists minded their own business. Then she wanted to know—out of idle curiosity—what answer I had made.

"I didn't make any, Margherita. It's not so easy for a man to suddenly tell people why he married his wife."

Margherita looked at me sternly.

"I should have thought it would be very easy," she said. "Unless the man's such a dunce he gets married without even knowing why. Since you married me, and not some other woman, you must have had a reason."

"That's what the woman on the telephone said. I certainly must have had a reason. But the fact is, taken unawares like that, I couldn't remember what it was."

"Do you remember now?" asked Margherita, with heavy sarcasm in her voice.

I tried to cast my mind back to the happy days of my youth, to relive my first meeting with Margherita. But no light came to me.

Then I remembered that in those days I had the laudable custom of keeping a diary, so I went up to my studio to dig it out. I reread what I had written at the time about my meetings with Margherita, but there was nothing in the notes to tell me the precise reason why I had married her.

"Well?" said Margherita, when I came down again. "May we have the honor of knowing why you deigned to marry us?"

I shrugged.

"You don't know!" cried Margherita angrily. "You've never known! You married me just like that, for some trivial reason!"

Here I rebelled.

"What do you mean, some trivial reason? People don't get married for trivial reasons. I married you because I wanted a family, I wanted children, and all that! Those aren't trivial reasons!"

Margherita, however, was not intimidated by the tone of my voice.

"If you'd married some other woman, and not me, you still could have had a family, and children, and all that! The point is, why did you marry *me?*"

I replied that in the question of marriage the most important role is played by fate: marriages are made in heaven, and heaven must help them along. X is born to marry Y, and so when X meets Y, they marry, that's all.

"What a glorious tale of love and passion!" Margherita cried, with heavy sarcasm. "I really didn't know I'd married such a sentimental man. How happy I'll be to read in the newspaper: 'I married my wife because in her I found my Y.' "

"Very well, Margherita," I cried, somewhat annoyed, "if they'd gone to you instead of me, and if they'd asked you,

'Why did you marry your husband?' what would you have answered?"

"Simple," Margherita declared. "I'd have told them the most reasonable thing in the world: 'I married my husband because I couldn't marry some other woman's husband. Every woman marries her husband and every man marries his wife.'"

I tried to point out to her how very superficial her answer was.

"How nice it would be, Margherita," I said, "if that's the way it was. But the trouble is, all too often a man marries another man's wife, and a woman marries another woman's husband. That's why there are so many unhappy marriages that end in tragedy. Anyway, all you did was paraphrase what I already said about X and Y. Be a little more precise—tell me why you married me."

"Just a minute!" cried Margherita. "Let's not get things the wrong way around. I didn't marry you. You married me, and I let you marry me. The man has the responsibility in a marriage, because he takes the initiative. You have no right to put the responsibility for our marriage on me!"

I told her it was not a question of fixing the responsibility. Furthermore, if she hadn't let herself be married to me, I couldn't have married her. So why did she let herself be married to me and not to someone else?

Margherita's sigh was long and sad.

"So that's what I've come to, have I?" she cried. "After all my sacrifices, after bringing up two children, after creating a home, I'm reproached for having let myself marry him!"

"There are no reproaches, Margherita. But since you

were being so sarcastic because I couldn't say why I'd married you, I've asked you to try saying why you married me."

Margherita rose. She went to the window to look out at the infinite. Then she turned.

"Giovannino," she said, "There must be some exact, precise reason why you married me and why I let you marry me. If we had no reason, then our marriage makes no sense, and our children are not the result of our union but of chance. They might just as well be other people's children."

"That, no," I objected. "They belong to us."

"In a physical sense," replied Margherita sadly. "But that's all. For if our marriage isn't reasonable, and therefore right, then how can the product of our marriage be either reasonable or right? Today, Giovannino, you admitted, after all these years, that you had no particular reason for marrying me, and you still don't realize that I let you marry me because, above all, I had confidence in you, I was sure that when you asked me to marry you, you had thought it over very carefully. Now we're faced with the fact that we've built a house without a foundation. We've taken the sum of our addition to be correct without knowing what the numbers were that we were adding. Margherita plus Giovannino, we said, make six. Then we multiplied six by two and got twelve. But what value does the result have if we don't really know whether Margherita plus Giovannino make six, or if they make seven or four? Don't you realize our children might be only a mistake—the result of another mistake?"

She sounded very discouraged, and I tried to reassure her.

"Don't complicate our marriage, Margherita, by getting it mixed up with arithmetic. We have two definite facts: one is, I married you; and the other is, I married you for a good reason. I'm not a man who makes decisions lightly. I know myself rather well. So all we have to do is think the thing over, calmly, and we'll get to the heart of the matter."

So we thought the thing over, calmly, beginning at the beginning again.

"Why did I marry you, Margherita? Let's consider all the possible answers. Did I marry you for money?"

"Absolutely not," declared Margherita.

"Or because I was captivated by your beauty?"

Here Margherita may have thought she detected a note of sarcasm in my voice.

"Time passes," she replied, somewhat apprehensively, "and age withers. A decision based on present-day reality couldn't possibly be valid. One must remember how things were then."

I got down the big album, and we looked conscientiously at all the pictures of Margherita then.

"Well, no," she said finally, "I wasn't beautiful in the common sense of the word—though there was certainly something about me. However, even though I don't know what your aesthetic criteria were, I think we may exclude the possibility that you married me because you were captivated by my beauty."

"Now, don't be disheartened," I said. "Couldn't it be that I was conquered by your liveliness and your wit, by your learning and intelligence?"

Margherita considered herself as a young girl, then shook her head.

"Frankly, no," she said.

Still, I remained convinced that there was a reason—if only we could isolate it. There was, therefore, no reason to be discouraged. Let each of us, I said, think about it for a while; then we would talk the various possibilities over.

A curtain of silence fell between us.

A few minutes later, from the other room, came the voice of Albertino: "What do you think, why did he marry her?"

"I can't imagine," replied the Pasionaria. "Maybe he wasn't very bright when he was young."

"No, that isn't it," protested Albertino. "I've looked at all the old notebooks and report cards he keeps in that green box, and I know he was intelligent because he got good marks in everything except mathematics."

"As though that made any difference!" The Pasionaria snickered. "When people marry, marks don't count. What I think is, he married her because she was older than he was, and so she was sharper."

Albertino continued to defend me.

"Don't be dumb!" he said. "A friend of mine's father was a good friend of ours, and he said that even when Papa was young, he was always on the ball."

"So why did he marry her? You heard what they said— not for her money, not for her beauty, not for her intelligence. He married her because he wasn't very bright when he was young."

Albertino made no immediate reply. Evidently he was thinking over his sister's unanswerable logic.

"Maybe," he said at last, "she wasn't very bright either."

"What I think is," the Pasionaria concluded, "they got married because they were both a little dumb."

There was a silence.

Then came the voice of Albertino again. "But what if he'd married someone else instead of her . . . ?" "Or," said the Pasionaria, "if she'd married someone else?"

There must have been a whirlwind of weighty considerations scuttering through Albertino's head. After a time—after, presumably, the inner turmoil was resolved —Albertino communicated the result to the Pasionaria.

"If he'd married someone else, and if she'd married someone else, whose children would we be?"

The Pasionaria gave a deep sigh. "Maybe we wouldn't even have been brother and sister."

"Maybe," Albertino added, "we wouldn't even have known each other."

"Just as well, then," cried the Pasionaria with a sigh of relief, "that she married him and he married her. It's better to be the children of parents, even if they're not so wonderful, than to be the children of strangers. Strangers make me sick."

At that, they went out to wreak heaven knows what havoc; and Margherita spoke: "They're probably right. You married me because you were a little stupid, and I married you because I was a little stupid. At any rate, it's better the way it is. If we'd each married someone else, whose children would our children be?"

"It's frightening to think about," I replied quite honestly.

When the woman telephoned from the magazine the next day, Margherita answered. "My husband says he married me for obvious reasons."

"That's not much of an answer," said the woman.

"Everyone gets married as best he can," Margherita replied. "The important thing is that a man marry his wife so his children don't fall into the hands of strangers."

"Strangers make me sick," grunted the Pasionaria, who happened to be passing.

THE 136 EXPRESS

"I often think about the engineer," I said, unintentionally aloud, "of the 136 express."

The children were reading, and Margherita was watching the flames dancing in the fireplace.

"Pay attention, children," said Margherita, "your father's mind is wandering again."

I was sorry I had spoken aloud, but fortunately the children had apparently not heard me, and Margherita did not seem to care much one way or the other.

After a few minutes of pleasant silence, the voice of the Pasionaria was heard. "Who was he, that engineer?"

"What engineer?" I murmured.

"Of the 136 express," said Albertino.

"None of your business," I replied. "He was just a railroad engineer like a thousand others."

"What happened to him?" asked the Pasionaria.

"Nothing!" I cried. "What do you think happened to him?"

"I know," said Margherita. "You were in an accident on Sunday when you went to Milan by train instead of driving."

"I wasn't in any accident! The engineer of the 136 is my own business—he's the hero of a little story I'd like to write some day, and it all happened years ago. That's all. It couldn't possibly be of the slightest interest to you."

"In that case," said the Pasionaria coldly, "you oughtn't to have mentioned it in the first place. It's like I showed you a piece of cake and then ate it myself."

"Don't go on with it," Margherita warned her. "Let him keep his old story. Tonight I'll tell you a hundred stories about railroad engineers."

"Yes," Albertino remarked cautiously, "but I'd like to hear the story of that particular man."

So I had to give in.

"All right," I said, "I'll tell you the story of the engineer of the 136. And it won't have the slightest meaning for you because it's not your kind of story."

"Are there any off-color situations?" asked Margherita.

"There are never off-color situations in my stories!" I replied indignantly. "I said it isn't your kind of story because the only person it could have any meaning for is me."

But they were waiting in silence, and so I began the story.

"Every time he took train number 136 out of the station, the engineer asked himself the same question: 'Will it happen again this time?' He could hear his heart beating as he asked himself: 'Will it happen again this time as it has every other time?'

"For two years now, whenever the 136 reached the curve at milepost 18, something happened that made the engineer more and more curious every time it happened.

"As the train approached the curve, it slowed down, and as it passed, at this reduced speed, the little white house that stood some fifty yards from the foot of the escarpment, the engineer used to see the shutters of the second window on the second floor being opened. Then a young woman leaned out and waved at him."

"I see," Margherita interrupted, "that it's a silly and probably immoral story—a story the children shouldn't hear."

"My story," I said, "is as proper as it can be."

"Waving at a passing train from a window," said the Pasionaria, "is that supposed to be wrong?"

I resumed my narrative.

"When the train, then, reached the curve, a young and beautiful girl leaned out of the second window of the second floor of the little house and waved her arm and smiled. For two years now, she had done this every time the train passed; and for two years, the engineer had responded by waving his cap.

"This constantly repeated episode had become, by now, an obsession with the engineer, and he thought about the girl at milepost 18 even when he wasn't on the train.

"The engineer was not happy. He was unmarried and lived with an old aunt who loved him very dearly; he had no worries, and there was no reason why he should not have gone on living his peaceful life—save for the terrible monotony of it.

"His only diversion was the girl at the curve. But how long would even this go on being a diversion?

"For the fact that it had been happening for two years made it seem as though it would go on forever—and become, therefore, just one more aspect of the general boredom of life.

"Then, one day, something unexpected happened at the curve. The train had slowed down, as usual, when, with a sudden squealing of the brakes, it came to a halt.

"A man slipped down from the train and disappeared into a little wood that stood near the escarpment.

"This created more than a little confusion, because the man who had jumped from the train was the engineer. After a few minutes, the conductor began to make inquiries, and eventually the train pulled away with the fireman at the controls.

"When the train had disappeared, the engineer came out of hiding and stood looking at the little white house.

"The beautiful young girl was still at the window: she had watched the engineer jump from the train and run into the thicket.

"She went on smiling as he walked toward the little white house.

"When he was below the window, he looked up.

" 'I hope,' he said, 'you will permit someone who is unknown to you to—' "

" 'But you are not unknown to me,' said the girl cheerfully. 'In fact, I've known you for two years. You're the engineer of the 136 express.'

"The driver spread his hands.

" 'Let's rather say I was. After what happened a few

minutes ago, I don't think I'll ever be again as long as I live.'

"The girl looked sad.

" 'What a pity,' she said with a sigh. 'A great pity. For I liked the engineer of the 136 express so very much. . . . And now that it's no longer you, will the train not pass here any more?'

" 'It will pass all right, as always, but with another engineer in my place.'

"The girl clapped her hands with joy.

" 'I can't wait for tomorrow to come,' she cried, 'so I can see the new engineer of the 136. Do you think he will be as handsome and charming as you?'

" 'That I couldn't say,' said the driver. 'However, I would like you to take note of the fact that I am not dead, and if I was handsome and charming half an hour ago, I must be so still.'

" 'I liked the engineer of the 136 express so very much,' said the girl. 'And you're no longer the engineer of the 136.'

"The engineer now looked at the girl for the last time and discovered that seen close-up she was nothing like what he thought when he saw her from the cab of the locomotive.

" 'Well, well,' he murmured, 'I'm afraid, with all our talk, it's grown very late.' He touched the visor of his cap. 'Goodbye,' he said.

" 'Goodbye,' said the girl, withdrawing from the window and closing the shutters."

There was a silence. The story was ended, but for a time everyone waited for me to go on. At last the Pasionaria said: "And him?"

"He went away."

"Where?" asked Albertino.

I shrugged, and concluded my story.

"He didn't go anywhere. He just wandered around the countryside and soon learned to live on nothing, like all the other vagabonds in the world. He wandered around the countryside following the railroad tracks. When he heard a train coming, he would hide in a thicket to watch the train go by, and then disappear.

"And even now, now that years and years have passed, the hobo who was once the engineer of the 136 express lives on in the same way."

The Pasionaria sighed. "Poor thing! I feel sorry for him."

"Me too," said Albertino.

"And the story," Margherita remarked, "is less improper than might have been expected. The moral of it—which, according to your father, is so profound and difficult none of us is capable of understanding it—is in fact lucid and clear: youth and beauty count for nothing in a woman."

"That would be convenient," said the Pasionaria, "for some people."

Margherita withered her with a glance, then went on: "What counts in a woman is heart. And heart, unlike youth and beauty, doesn't leap at once to the eye. But I pity the man who loses his head to a girl because of her youth and her beauty without making sure that her spiritual gifts are equal to the superficial, vulgar, outward physical ones."

The Pasionaria was silent for a moment, then she said: "Well, if it's a question of youth and beauty, why is Papa always thinking about the engineer of the 136 express?"

"The explanation is that you are an impertinent little fool!" cried Margherita. "You tell her, Giovannino, whether I'm right or not."

I shook my head.

"Margherita," I said, "you are right to rebuke your daughter for her disrespectful and untimely sarcasm. But as to the rest of it, you're wrong. I think of the engineer of the 136 express because I *am* the engineer of the 136. Ever since the first man ran away, I have been running that train—and when it gets to the curve, I'm the one the girl waves at."

"What a way to talk in front of your children!" cried Margherita indignantly. "You ought to be ashamed! And is that what you do when you say you're going to Milan to work?'"

"Yes, Margherita, every time the train approaches that fatal curve and I see the beautiful girl waving at me, I think, 'Next time I'll stop the thing and jump out.' I am weary, Margherita, and my work seems to grow ever more difficult and unrewarding, and I'd like to forget everything and accept the invitation I have read all these years in the smile of the pretty girl at the window. But I never do, for I remember the story of the man I replaced. I don't stop the train, I don't jump out—I'm afraid of ending up as he did. But I feel that maybe one day I won't be afraid any more."

Margherita shook her head vigorously.

"Not you, Giovannino," she said, "you can't. The other engineer lived alone with his old aunt, and had no children."

"Don't be vulgar, Margherita! What have children got to do with it?"

"When a man has children, his chief duty is to go on working for the rest of his life."

"Oh, I'm not saying I'd become a hobo. There are plenty of things I could do!"

"A man's chief duty is to do his own work, not someone else's."

"But suppose I've come to the conclusion that what I've been doing up to now is not my own work?"

"So much the worse for you, Giovannino. It's too late now. For too many years now, whether in good faith or bad, you've been playing with words: equivocation has become the cross you have to bear, and you'll have to bear it to the end. So go on, Giovannino, go on riding the 136 express. I'll be the fireman at your side."

The Pasionaria gave a wicked laugh. "And she's the one who never rides in trains because she's afraid of tunnels!"

"We're not talking about riding trains," Margherita replied fiercely. "We're talking in allegory."

Then she turned to me. "Giovannino, do you remember that old poster you have in your studio? The one where the locomotive is just coming out of the Simplon tunnel, and to the west, in the enormous plain of Lombardy, you can just glimpse the tallest spire of the Cathedral at Milan?"

"Yes, Margherita."

"Well, then, I'll be the one on the left and you the one on the right."

The Pasionaria, who knew the photograph, handed out some motherly advice. "You better put heavy sweaters on. Otherwise, by the time you get to Lodi, you'll both be dead of pneumonia."

"You be quiet," said Margherita. "Allegories can travel without clothes even in winter."

Margherita is right: the years don't weigh heavily on an allegory. But I am not an allegory—and I still think that some day, when I get to that curve, I'll stop the train and jump out.

And I'll continue on my way *pedibus calcantibus.*